HOLLYWOOD CHURCH

Short Stories and Poems

by

WENDY RAINEY

VAINGLORY PRESS

LOS ANGELES

November 2015

Second Edition

January 2018

VAINGLORY PRESS

Los Angeles, California

ISBN-13: 978-0692556733

ISBN-10: 0692556737

Please contact the author for permissions at
vainglorypress@gmail.com

After reading these powerful, though deeply-disturbing stories and poems, Southern California will never be the same for me. Wendy Rainey has redefined L.A. Noir and given the grotesque entwined with the lyrical it's own unique place in the California literary canon. I'm full of admiration for the author's gifts, and sense there's a lot more to come!
-Edward Field
Author of *After the Fall: Poems Old and New.*

This book is the culmination of a lifetime of writing and of sharing that work in professional workshops with her peers. It is the signature book that we have all been waiting for, the one we know will vault her into the most prominent ranks of her generation. It is also a classic of SoCal literature. I have known Wendy since her student years and known her work over this same period of time. There is no way to overstate the joy I share with her in the emergence of this eminent literary document. It is an instant classic. She is as at home in surrealistic voyaging as in her gritty, soulful neo-naturalism. A literary star is born!
-Gerald Locklin, author of over one hundred volumes of poetry, fiction, and literary essays. Described by Charles Bukowski as "One of the great undiscovered talents of our time." Author: *Poets and Pleasure Seekers*

This collection of stories and poems is brilliant and brutal. Hollywood without the façade. Wendy Rainey is the kind of storyteller I've been waiting to read. If anyone asks me about a new writer to consider, she is the one.
-Nico Soultanakis, film producer. Credits include *The Cell*, *Immortals*, *Mirror Mirror*, co-producer and co-writer of *The Fall*

Marilyn Monroe said Hollywood is the kind of place where they offer you $3000 for a kiss and 50 cents for your soul. She liked to say she always held out for the 50 cents. In Wendy Rainey's collection "Hollywood Church," earnest working-class people – nannies, former prostitutes, truckers and more -- struggle against a glittering glamorous lie to hold onto their souls and find (and maybe keep) a little tenderness. She shines a light on the underbelly of human nature in stories like "Dinosaur Killing Asteroid," where a high-powered successful Hollywood executive can't bear her daughter's love. Her solution is to drug her loving, boisterous four-year-old to keep the kid from being a nuisance. In other moments, a statuette of Big Boy becomes a reminder of infidelity and Hollywood Boulevard becomes the Arizona Desert. The Hollywood Wendy Rainey shows us is a grim one, far from the Technicolor dream. "You will see a vacancy there that we have mistaken for greatness," she writes. But that Vacancy sign flickers on and off, promising hope. The nanny stands up to the mother's cruelty. The trucker remembers beauty. And, in a lovely lyric poem, a swarm of Monarch butterflies descends on a freeway overpass. There is tension in this book, a struggle for beauty and hope against the odds. Wendy Rainey writers like a modern-day Jean Rhys. In "Hollywood Church," she shows us something true about ourselves and our world and helps us realize what our souls are truly worth.

-Lori Jakiela- author of *Belief is its Own Kind of Truth, Maybe*

Acknowledgements

Grateful acknowledgment is made to the editors of the following publications in which these works or earlier versions of them previously appeared: *These Pages Speak*, edited by Hiram Sims (World Stage Press, 2016). *Dryland Literary Journal, Chiron Review, Carnival Literary Journal, Cultural Weekly, Silver Birch Press, Paper and Ink Literary Zine, Truth and Lies that Press for Life*, anthology edited by Connie Hershey, *The New Los Angeles Poets*, anthology edited by Jack Grapes.

Thank you to Jack Grapes, Gerald Locklin, Alexis Rhone Fancher, Michael Hathaway, Curtis Cummings, and Barbara Cummings. Thank you to the students in Jack Grapes' classes over the years who have been so supportive. Thank you to California Poets in the Schools Program for encouraging me to write at such a young age.

for Curtis Cummings

from an ordinary corpse on fire

TABLE OF CONTENTS

Hollywood Success

There was nothing to suggest greatness
unless you counted the vastness of the Arizona desert
which doubled as a movie set.
The horse she rode in on was an anguished creature,
caught and trapped in a faraway land
and brought back to Burbank to be whipped and broken
and led away in chains.
If you look into that beast's eyes you will know what it is
to be terrified,
not of anything in particular
but the sheer monotony of the carnival carousel,
the sea of eyes
and the horrible laughter of the popcorn munchers,
the screamers,
the peeing and sweating mob—
the way they feed on the meat of the beast.
They want the beast to be funnier,
they want the beast to be bloodier,
they want the beast to kill or be killed,
they want to eat the flesh of the beast and become the beast
but they cannot,
these multitudes who demand so much from the beast
but give nothing in return.
And she, the girl with knees that bend
in front of powerful men
and a head that bops like a turkey to their members.
She who rides the beast with a gloved hand and an orchid
between her legs
that spread onscreen.
She with a body into which they all want to dip their fingers
and taste and eat
and rip open with the juices running down their chins.

And you,
who work in offices, you who are teachers, lawyers, mechanics,
and dentists,
you mothers with a baby at your breast,
you who hate your lives,
you who are children afraid of becoming adults,
you who left your wife for someone else's,
you who left Nebraska because you were bored—
when you go to that dark temple to prey
look up into her eyes
and you will see a vacancy there
that we have mistaken for greatness—
as vast as the Arizona desert.

Juliette at 16

Juliette told me that when she was 15 she lived in a room on 4th and San Pedro. She said she lived there with a bunch of other girls. She had needle tracks all up her legs and arms, and one day she wandered around downtown in her nightgown, barefoot, with a black eye, and a busted lip. The police picked her up, questioned her, and brought her back to her parents affluent home in Belmont Shore. I never asked her any questions. We were both baggers at Ralph's across the street from Cal State Long Beach where I attended college. While we collected carts from the parking lot, Juliette would often disclose details about what her life had been like in downtown. "There were six of us living in this room on the second floor. Three girls worked there during the day and the other three would have to work the streets. Then at night the girls who had worked the streets would have to work in the apartment, and the girls that worked in the apartment would have to work the streets. It's like we almost never stopped working except for about six or seven hours out of the day when we were allowed to sleep and eat. I got beaten up a lot after sex. And they wanted me to do all kinds of really weird stuff. Like extreme, sick stuff and it was just…" she was shaking her head and biting her nails as her voice trailed off. "Do you hate me?" she asked, looking at me, "Do you think I'm scum?" "No, I don't hate you, Juliette," I said as I pushed a long line of carts up the parking lot and into the front door of Ralph's. "I don't think you're scum."

She was blonde-haired and blue-eyed. She couldn't have weighed more than a hundred pounds. I wondered how she could even still be alive after all that. And where were her parents while all this was happening? I noticed she was strong, though. When she put her mind to it she could work faster than most of the boys. She liked to make a game out of connecting as many carts as she could. Customers would stop and watch her push an impossibly long line of carts through the parking lot, some offering to help her. She would smile and say, "No, thank you. I have it under control."

"I was a whore," she said to me one time in the breakroom. She sat on the chair with her knees tucked up under her chin, eating a peanut butter and jelly sandwich and slurping her milk through a straw, "I was a fucking whore." "I know, Juliette," I told her. "But the best thing for you to do right now is to just do normal stuff. Pretend everything is normal," I said, looking her in the eye. "And then after some time passes, things *will* seem normal. Anyway, let's get back to the carts before we get into trouble. He thinks we yack too much." I motioned with my head to the the supervisor we could see through the window. "He thinks we can't handle it." "Can't handle it?

We work at a Super Market! What's to handle? Screw you, Baldy!" she said, glancing in his direction and throwing her sandwich in the trash. I got up, threw my styrofoam cup of Top Ramen noodles in the can and said, " Let's show that old fart how it's done!"

For the next several months Juliette blossomed. She gained weight and her thin blonde hair grew into a lustrous mane that flowed out behind her as she collected carts. Her acne cleared up. She even grew ¾ of an inch in height. She won a cash award for the fastest bagger in the region, and she passed her high school equivalency exam.

Then one day two police officers came into Ralph's. I saw them go up to the service counter and speak to the supervisor. The supervisor said something and then looked in my direction, motioning me to come over to the counter. One of the policeman said, "Do you know anything about the whereabouts of Juliette Jameson?" "No, I don't," I said. Juliette had uncharacteristically not shown up for her shift that afternoon. "Why didn't she show up for work today? What happened to her?" I asked, looking at both of the officers. "That'll be all, Miss" one of the policeman said. I looked at my supervisor, "Bob, what happened to Juliette? You know she would never just not show up for work without calling or anything." Bob looked as worried as I was. "I know," he said, shaking his head and biting his lip. He let out a sigh and looked at the schedule in front of him, tapping his pen on the counter. "We need you on carts now." He motioned for me to go back to work.

After work that day I made a chocolate cake in the makeshift kitchen in my one room apartment. I emptied the contents of the cake mix in a large bowl and added water, oil, and eggs, mixing it together and pouring the batter into a pan. I baked it at 350 for forty-five minutes. After the cake was finished baking I let it cool, placing paper towels over it to keep the roaches off. I spread white butter cream frosting on it, making jagged lines, bumps, and slashes with a knife. When I was finished I sat down in front of the cake and stared at it for two hours, thinking about the stories Juliette had told me about her life. I remembered that the room she lived in in downtown had blinds that were always shut and dark blue curtains pulled over the blinds. There were cracks in the walls and chipped and bumpy plaster on the ceiling. Juliette said that when she stared at the lines and cracks in the ceiling she could see a lion and a machete that ran the length of the room. She would have dreams that the lion was chasing her down an alley off of 6th street, and that it would trap her in a dead end. She would grab the machete and stab it in the gut, its blood spilling out of it and into the gutter. I fell asleep that night thinking about Juliette running down 6th street in her nightgown, the lion chasing her down an alley that led to a dead end.

I found out the next day that Juliette had shot her father three times (in the hand, foot, and shoulder) in her bedroom, and then fled the scene. The police found her sitting under a tree, smoking a cigarette at Whaley Park. Her face and clothes were splattered with her father's blood.

She was being held in custody. It was a few weeks later that I read in the paper that the charges against her were dropped, and that her father (who was the president of a bank) was arrested for having sexually abused her since she was three.

Juliette sent me a postcard from San Diego a few days before her seventeenth birthday:

I'm OK. I live with my aunt and uncle now. They're making me go to a psychiatrist like three hours a day. I have to take antidepressants and shit. Whatever. I'm going to be a marine biologist, or a sculptor, or a surgical nurse maybe. I don't know yet, but I'll write you again in a couple of weeks. Hey, remember when you said that I should try to do normal things and after some time passes things will start to seem normal? You told me to pretend that things are normal. Well, sometimes that works. I guess that's what everybody does.

Pretending,

Juliette

That was the last I ever heard from Juliette.

Dinosaur-Killing Asteroid

Three years ago, I was working as a nanny for Barbara B. I would eventually end up calling her The Barbarian of Beverly Hills. She was and still is an agent and producer in Hollywood. Before she would even hire me I had to sign a confidentiality clause. But you know what? Fuck that shit. I'm just as unscrupulous as anyone in this little Sodom and Gomorrah. Nothing is confidential, so you're going to get the straight scoop from me. I have to say, though, I enjoyed taking care of Celeste, Barbara's four-year-old daughter. Only I guess she'd be seven now. Celeste could really make me laugh, and she was smart as hell. And she had all this curly red hair that flew all over the place all the time because she was always running around like a monkey. Most four-year-olds are bundles of energy, but that kid never stopped moving. Barbara was fond of saying, "My daughter is like a Tasmanian Devil on speed, crack, and heroin." When Celeste would have a question, her mother never listened. She would roll her eyes and say, "What is it now, Groinfruit? Fruit of my groin." She never bothered answering any of Celeste's questions. If Celeste persisted in asking questions, Barbara would put on jazz or symphony music to drown out Celeste's voice. I've got to hand it to Celeste though, she never quit. She never lost heart when she was ignored. When she continued not to get a response from her mother she would make up her own answers to some of the questions she'd asked. I liked Celeste, partly because I knew that nothing was going to be easy for her, and the way I figured it, she was going to need all the encouragement she could get. Don't get me wrong. I didn't applaud every time the kid took a shit. And more than a few times I was relieved to be getting away from her at the end of the day. Relieved to be retreating back to my apartment where I could rest up for the next day's assault to my senses. But I kept the child safe when I could and I listened to her when she was in my care. She delighted as much as she exhausted me. Ultimately though, I was only a bystander, watching the horror of childhood unfold as it does for all of us. This is not a vindictive story from a disgruntled nanny. I'm writing this now because I still wake up at night sometimes thinking about Celeste and the way she looked the last time I saw her. It was as if a calm had come over her. A horrible calm that I knew wasn't right. And there was something about the world I lived in that would never seem right to me again.

The first week I started working as Celeste's nanny I realized that she needed a pair of earplugs. I made the mistake of entering the Beverly Hills mansion with my charge in tow. We took the elevator up to the third floor, walked through the corridor, and entered the office through the open door while her mother was talking shop on the phone: "What the fuck do you want me to do, Albert? They've got me by the short hairs. And I've already taken it up the ass from Ronnie and those cunt lappers at Miramar. So, what the fuck do you want me to do here, Al?" I put both of my hands over Celeste's ears but she wiggled away and ran straight to the bear-skin rug that she liked to roll around on. "What did you just mumble under your breath, Albert? What? Oh, blow me, fucker. We'll see who's sucking who's asshairs when this deal finally goes down. Oh, yeah, baby? Yeah? Well, you never bothered doing that to me when we were actually married. Oh, that's right. If you had only succeeded in finding my warm, gooey spot we might still be together, blah, blah, blah, you boring little puddle of fuck." Barbara slammed the phone down just as she turned to greet us. "Oh, girls, girls!" Her arms reached out as if to encircle us both. "I'm so glad you're here." She looked at me, her smile fading, as she eyeballed me up and down. "Katherine, that's an awfully sheer blouse, dear. And that skirt is awfully short. And please remember that I never want to see you in open-toed shoes." She waited for my response. I mumbled something about the heat wave we were experiencing and the triple-digit temperature. But I realized the heat hadn't fazed her because she kept her office at a frigid 62 degrees at all times. The wave of cold air felt good at first but after a few moments I started to shiver. "Perhaps I can have you put on one of my cardigans for modesty's sake?" She threw a white sweater at me which I immediately donned, grateful for the warmth it provided. "That's better. Let's try to keep our attire a little more business-like in the future, shall we?" She turned to watch Celeste climb the ladder up the bookcase, pull out books on the top shelf and throw them across the room. My daughter has certain simian characteristics," Barbara said. I had my hands on her instantly, grabbing her, and guiding her down the ladder. I put her on the couch and handed her a coloring book and some colors to work with. She threw the box of crayons in the air and the coloring book on the floor and ran over to and rolled around on the bear-skin rug again. "What's a puddle of fuck, Mommy? What's asshairs?" The phrase, "Blow me, fucker," came out of her little rosebud mouth three times as she rolled off the bear-skin rug and onto the marble floor, her head coming dangerously close to a bronze sculpture. I raced over to where she had rolled, picked her up off the floor and set her down on the couch again. This time I reached into my bag and handed her a kaleidoscope. She was enthralled for all of thirty seconds, then she ran to the fireplace, grabbed the fire iron, swung it around the room, and thrashed the dead embers. I ran over to her, took the fire iron from her hand; "We don't play with the poker, Celeste. It's not safe," I said.

Barbara's landline rang and she picked it up. "Hey Jeremy. How's the rewrite coming along? Uh huh, uh uh, oh my, that's horrible, I see. Yes, oh yes, I understand, dear. Look, the reason I'm about to bend you over a log and shove my dick up your ass is because I need you to finish by the deadline, motherfucker. So, I don't wanna hear your whining. Stop worrying about the plumbing and the delivery. I don't care if your house is flooding with water and wifey poo is going into labor. I suggest you get to high ground, call a midwife, and bang out that piece in the next few hours. Just filter out all the crap that's going on in your shitty little life right now. Don't overthink this, Jeremy. Just bang it out. Get it on all fours and bang it till she screams like a bitch in heat. Then slap her on the ass and send her out the door. She's not staying for eggs and toast, ya know?" She took a drink from the glass of scotch and water on her desk and tossed back her long, dark hair. "Look, I've got my child and the nanny with me right now so I've got to go spend some quality time with them. You may not believe this kid, but you're one of the few writers I actually like. So I'm gonna give you a break. Instead of that piece being due by midnight, I'm making it due at 6 sharp tomorrow morning. Get that rewrite to me by tomorrow morning at 6 or consider yourself fired."

She slammed the phone down and turned to us, smiling. "So girls, what have you been doing so far today?" She looked out the window. "It's such a glorious day, Katherine, I want you to take Celeste to the park and wear her down. Have her do summersaults, pushups, hopscotch, leapfrog, jump rope, hula-hoop, ring around the rosie, get her on the monkey bars, the jungle gym, and the swing. She can climb trees if she wants. Have her kick the soccer ball, make her run laps if you have to, and here's her swimsuit. Tell her she's a water ballerina and she'll be in that pool for two hours pirouetting and arabesquing or whatever." Barbara threw a green one-piece suit with a built in tutu at me. "Just give her a hardcore workout, know what I mean? You've probably noticed that she has an over abundance of energy and she needs to be worn out physically to be manageable. I see you're doing a fabulous job, though, Kate. I commend you on your stamina. Not only are you watching her like a hawk, but evidently you've been able to prevent her from injuring herself every time she performs some death-defying stunt which is like every five fucking minutes." She laughed, lit up a cigarette and took a drag. "More power to you if you can keep her out of Cedars Emergency Room. That's more than I was ever able to do. When a 911 situation occurs, and it will, here's her medical and insurance information." Barbara handed me a paper with all the pertinent addresses and phone numbers. "Thank you, Barbara. I'll keep this in my purse," I said to her. "Good idea. You'll probably need it just like all her other nannies did." Barbara looked over at Celeste who was wrestling her gigantic stuffed rabbit. Celeste picked up the rabbit and threw it against the wall several times. She grabbed its head and bashed it on the floor. Then she got on top of it and started biting its face and ears. "Blow me, fucker!" She screamed. "You know," Barbara said, "when Celeste was a toddler I got so sick of changing her. I had to do it a couple of times a day. She had three nannies that worked in eight hour shifts. But sometimes the nanny would have to use the restroom herself or have a bite to eat or have a nervous breakdown or whatever, so I would help out. And I got to thinking wouldn't it be great if kids could just change themselves? You know, like a self-cleaning-oven, only it would be a self-cleaning kid." "A self- cleaning kid?" I asked. "Yes, it would be a lot more convenient if they could just do the dirty work themselves. Hell, I don't know, maybe they could just eat their own poop and we wouldn't even have the smell or mess to clean up at all." I stared at her, wondering if she was drunk. She started to laugh; "I had you going, didn't I? I fucking had you going!" She threw her head back and laughed and took another drink from her glass of Scotch.

The next day Celeste and I came back to the mansion after I picked her up from her over-priced, Reggio preschool in Beverly Hills. It was a school where the teachers were not allowed to use the word, "no" to kids. I could already hear Barbara on the phone so I waited in the corridor with Celeste. "I want bubbles, Katherine," Celeste said. "No, Celeste. No bubbles in the house," I said. "But I want bubbles NOW!" Celeste screamed. "Sit down, Celeste." I picked her up and put her in a chair and handed her the books she liked to read. She threw the books on the floor and screamed, "Give me my bubbles now!" "No bubbles, Celeste. Listen to me. You're the kid. I'm the adult. I'm in charge. Now sit down and be quiet. You are not getting bubbles in the house." I think she was so stunned to have an adult actually yell at her and tell her what to do that it rendered her mute for a few minutes. She sat there with her mouth open, staring at me while I listened through the door.

"Yeah, I'm really excited to have you on board, Simon," I could hear Barbara saying. "How's that pretty, young wife of yours? Oh, really? She's due in two weeks? Oh, how exciting for you two. Yes, yes, children are a blessing, aren't they? Hhhmm? Oh, indeed it's why were put on God's green earth. There is no greater privilege than to be a parent. Yes, Simon, I too will continue to keep all three of you in my prayers." I could hear Barbara hang up the phone. I turned to Celeste and said, "The coast is clear. Let's go in." I knocked on the door and Barbara opened it. Celeste came charging in. She grabbed her mother's waist and hugged her: "I love you, Mommy! I love you!" "Gawd, I just got off the phone with the world's biggest perv," Barbara said, with her arms around Celeste. "Simon used to organize orgies for studio executives." She laughed. "Orgies with hookers, actresses, models. But he's sixty-nine now with a 28-year-old pregnant wife. He's all into Christianity now. Fucking Hypocrite. But who cares. He's rich." She focused her attention on both of us as I helped Celeste get out her Legos. "So, how are you two getting along today?" Just then her phone rang. She went to her desk to answer it. "What do you want now, asswipe? No, I'm only *half* Jewish, get it right, Dick Breath. So when are you gonna come over and see your Jew kid, Albert? When? She's been asking for you. Okay, but you better make good on that. "Celeste," Barbara called out in a sing-song voice, "Albert is coming to see you tomorrow. He has promised." Celeste got up off the floor where she had been building a helicopter with Legos. "Albert is coming tomorrow. Albert is coming! I love Albert. Albert! Albert! Albert!" Celeste was jumping up and down. "Albert, I wanna talk to Albert! I wanna talk to Albert!" She ran over to where Barbara was talking on the phone and tried to grab the receiver. Barbara pushed her hands away. Celeste grabbed the receiver again and Barbara pushed her forehead. She toppled to the floor. Gathering herself back up again, Celeste lunged for the receiver yet another time, but was pushed in the chest and fell backward onto the carpet, rolling away, screaming, "Albert! Albert! Albert!" Barbara turned her back to Celeste. "Hey, you know who I just got off the phone with?" Barbara said, "The Orgy Organizer, yeah, Simon. His family is Jewish. He was never a practicing Jew, but now the little freak has converted to Christianity, can you believe it?" Celeste, never one to give up easily, got up off the floor and sprinted toward her mother, tackling her and knocking the phone from her hand. Celeste grabbed the receiver and screamed into it, "Albert, I love you! Are you coming to see me tomorrow?" Barbara grabbed the phone from Celeste and held onto the bow on the back of her dress while she tried to wiggle away. They both started laughing when Celeste once again tried to grab the receiver and Barbara held it away from her. "Your daughter is attacking me, Albert. Talk to her." Barbara finally gave the receiver to Celeste who was out of breath by then. "Oh, Albert. I miss you. Oh, Albert are you coming to see me tomorrow? Are you bringing candy and presents like last time? Albert, I love you so much, oh, Albert." "I want you to take her to the library this afternoon," Barbara said to me. "She's on a dinosaur kick. Check out some dinosaur books for her. And then give her the royal workout at the park. You know the routine. Really wear her down. I want her good and tired before you bring her back here this evening. I mean I want her practically dead on her feet. Understand?" "Yes, I understand, Barbara." "Okay, good. Be back here by six, Katherine." "Will do," I said. Barbara went to the phone to collect Celeste who was speaking rapidly into the receiver. Barbara grabbed the receiver from Celeste and told her that she was going to the library and the park with nanny now. Celeste started to cry as we made our way to the door and then the front door and out to the car.

She was still crying when we got to the Beverly Hills Library, but she recovered as soon as I showed her a dinosaur picture book. Then I took her to the adult section and found a book on dinosaurs that had much more sophisticated illustrations. She was immediately enthralled. "Look Celeste," I pointed to an illustration of an asteroid crashing into Earth. "Scientists believe that a collision with a giant asteroid, about six miles across, changed the shape of life on Earth forever." I turned to her, "That asteroid crashed into Earth and killed all the dinosaurs. That's a dinosaur-killing asteroid." "Oooooohhhhhh, dinosaur-killing asteroid," Celeste murmured. She pointed to the next page: "Volcanoes!" "Yes, extensive volcanism occurred after the asteroid collided with Earth. Also, Celeste, the asteroid collision created so much dust that it blocked the sun's rays, darkening and chilling Earth, killing almost all the plants and animals. And when the dust finally settled, greenhouse gases created by the impact caused temperatures to skyrocket. Most of the plants and animals died on Earth at that time, including the dinosaurs." "Ooooooooohhhhhh, the dinosaurs died." Just then Celeste passed gas. "I farted!" "Let's use our library voice, Celeste,"

I said. She let out several more farts. "I can't help it," she said. "It's okay, Celeste," I smiled at her, giving her a nudge, and she burst into giggles. I noticed the librarian glaring at both of us as we walked up to the desk to check out the dinosaur books. Taking Celeste's hand, I glared back at her. Next, it was on to the park and pool where I wore the little girl out as instructed. For two hours I had her running laps around the park, doing pushups, sit ups, jumping jacks, handstands, summersaults, climbing trees, kicking the ball, rolling down the grassy hill, playing catch, tug of war, climbing on the jungle gym, going down the slide, swinging from the bars, hopscotch, jump rope, leapfrog, tetherball, dodge ball, and for an additional hour she swam the dog paddle in the shallow end and pretended to be a ballerina in her green tutu swimsuit. The weeks and months passed by in this way and I grew physically stronger from all the exercise Celeste required. I lost twenty pounds and toned my legs and and arms, and in general looked and felt better than I ever had.

Several months later, Barbara asked me to come to her office before I picked up Celeste from her preschool. She was with another showbiz type, Jean, who was probably about forty-five. They were just about to view a short film that had been delivered to her office. Barbara asked me to view it with them. It was about 20 minutes long. When the film was over, Barbara turned on the lights and said, "What do you think of the film, Katherine?" "You're asking the nanny?" Jean said. "She's a bright woman, Jean. What do you think, Kate? Is it too dark?" "Absolutely not," I said, looking at her. "I think it could be darker. If I were a writer I would do a rewrite and make the two characters even darker when they're talking about their spouses. And in the end I think we should actually *see* them each commit suicide. The problem with it, is that it isn't dark *enough*." "Oh, words of wisdom from Mary Fuckin' Poppins over here," Jean said. "It's nice to know that the average person can fancy themselves a writer." "In fact, Jean, my nanny is a writer and she's good." Barbara looked at me, "I Googled you yesterday, Katherine. I check up on you periodically. I want to know who's taking care of my kid. I read those short stories you had published online. Why didn't you tell me you have these hidden talents?" I stared at her. "Don't worry, you're not in trouble. Actually, I'm glad my kid is around someone talented. But tell me, do you think she's too hyper?" "You're asking me if Celeste is too hyper?" "Yes," Barbara said, "is Celeste too uncontrollable?" "The truth, Barbara?" I asked. "Yes, of course, the truth." "And you won't fire me for telling you the truth?" "Of course I won't fire you. Tell me the truth." "Well, I think the acorn doesn't fall too far from the tree. You're exactly alike, you and Celeste." Jean burst into laughter, "Well, that's telling her!" Barbara ignored Jean. "But when you take care of her aren't you completely exhausted at the end of the day?" "Of course I am, but that's to be expected. She's inexorable. She just keeps going," I said. "But do you think it's *normal* for a kid to just wear you down to a nub like that every day? Day-in and day-out? I mean I've seen other peoples' kids and they aren't nearly as active as Celeste." "Celeste is normal, Barbara," I said. "She just has a greater capacity for fun than most humans." "Well, more words of wisdom from Mary Poppins," Jean said, taking a sip from her glass of wine." That's Mary F. Poppins, Jean," I said, looking at her. "Touché'," Jean said, raising her glass to me. "Alright," Barbara said, "you can go now. Oh, by the way, Celeste has a doctor's appointment today, so I've decided to give you the day off. And I'm going to be staying home with her for the rest of the week. I want you to come back here next Monday at 12 noon."

I came back to the mansion at 12 the following Monday. Barbara told me that Celeste was in her room playing. The monitor was on Barbara's desk and I could see Celeste on the screen, playing quietly on the floor with her Legos. "Is Celeste sick?" I asked. "I remember you said that she had a doctor's appointment last week, and she looks so sedate sitting there. Is she feeling well?" "Yes, she's fine," Barbara said. "You can go up to her room and play and read. There's no need to go to the park and the pool today. You two can just play indoors. Read books to her and let her play with her toys. She'll probably take a nap soon." "Celeste has never taken a nap when I've cared for her." "She takes one now," Barbara said, turning to her desk and picking up the phone to make a call. "You can go up to her room. As I say, just play quietly today. You can take her outside in the backyard if you get bored." "Bored? Since when have I ever gotten bored around Celeste?" I asked. But Barbara was already on the phone talking to one of her writers or producers and I knew she couldn't hear me. I walked up the staircase to Celeste's room and walked in.

Celeste didn't get up to say hello. She just sat there playing with her Legos and staring at me. "Hey there, Celeste." I was surprised she didn't get up and run towards me like she usually did. "How are you today?" "Good," she said, looking at me. She turned back to her Legos and continued playing with them. "Do you want to go outside and go on your swing and your slide?" I asked. "Do you want to run around and I'll chase you and then we'll play hide and seek? Do you want to do summersaults on the lawn and roll down the grassy hill? Why don't we go check the backyard for dinosaurs? Maybe some of them aren't extinct." "No, I don't want to go outside," Celeste said, "I want to stay here." "Okay, we'll just stay here today." Celeste played all day with her toys by herself. She didn't talk much to me. She looked at picture books and listened to music and at one point she came over to where I was sitting and reading and put her hand on my leg. "I like you, Katherine," she said. "I like you too, Celeste. Are you feeling okay today? Why don't you want to go outside?" I asked. "I'm tired," is all Celeste said the rest of the day.

When it came time for me to leave, I stopped by Barbara's office and knocked on the door. She let me in. I could see the monitor on her desk. I could see Celeste on the screen. She was in the corner of her room, holding a doll. "Time for you to leave, Katherine? Okay, I'll be down there in a minute. How did things go today?" she asked. "Well, to tell you the truth, things were pretty strange today, Barbara. Why is Celeste so tired? Is she sick? She doesn't have any energy." "Celeste is fine," Barbara said.

"Don't worry about Celeste." "Well, I am worried, Barbara. She's not acting like herself. What's wrong with her?" "I repeat, Celeste is fine. It is not your concern, Katherine. I'll see you back here tomorrow at 1 PM. Celeste has another doctor's appointment tomorrow, so I don't need you until one." "Is Celeste on drugs?" I asked. "Are you drugging her? She's not acting normal." "Celeste has issues and those issues are being dealt with by a professional," Barbara said. "Now, I appreciate your concern, Katherine, but this is none of your affair." "What did you put her on? Some kind of sedative or Ritalin or something like that?" I asked. "Katherine, drop it. I'll see you tomorrow." She started walking me to the door. "This can't be legal, what you're doing. There's nothing wrong with Celeste other than she's an inconvenience for you." "Watch what you say, Katherine, I haven't fired you yet and I don't want to have to. You're a good nanny for my daughter. Drop this line of questioning now." "What you're doing can't be legal. It can't." I looked at her. "But it is legal," she said, smiling. "The doctors are helping me adjust her dosage. It might be that she is getting too much medication or not the right kind. We're figuring it out as we go." She turned from me and walked back to her desk. "How can you do this to your daughter, Barbara? There's nothing wrong with her. I've spent six months with her. She's a brilliant, healthy, loving little girl. Who are you to do this to anyone?" Barbara picked up a bottle of Scotch off her desk and threw it against the wall. She started walking towards me, her nostrils flaring. I was scared. "Who am I, you ask? Who am I?" She was standing so close to me I

31

could smell the whiskey on her breath. "I am a success. I am powerful. I am a winner. Everything you see here," she waved her arms in the air, "all of this materialized off the sweat of my back. I created my life from nothing. Nobody helped me with anything, okay? Nobody sent me to college, nobody asked me what I wanted to be when I grew up, nobody cared if I lived or died. It was all on me. I am self-made. I am the definition of success. I never ask anyone if it's okay to do something. Ya know what I'm saying? I just do it. I take what I want. That is who I am. Who the hell are you? That's what I'd like to know." Barbara took a few steps toward me. "You have the makings to be somebody, but you aren't doing enough to make that happen. I've seen your writing. I should hire you as a writer. But then I ask myself why, when she's such a good nanny and they're so much harder to find than writers. Do you even think about how you're wasting your time and energy? If you love kids so much then why don't you just fucking have your own? What are you doing here? And you're asking me who I am? Who the fuck are you?" "Listen Barbara, I have footage of you on my cell phone, pushing Celeste when she was trying to take the phone from you. Maybe the authorities would like to see my little home movie. Maybe you better rethink what you're doing to Celeste." She grabbed my phone, opened the window and threw it from the third story onto the concrete driveway below. I watched it smash to bits. I didn't actually have any footage of Celeste's and Barbara's phone antics. "That was a five-hundred-dollar phone," I said. "You're fired!" she said, "Leave now." She pointed to the door. "Thank you, Barbara, now I can collect unemployment." "Well, of course a weakling like you would," she said. I pointed my finger at her: "What about you, Barbara?" I was shaking by then. "What if someone had dulled you down with drugs when you were four years old? Would you have the juice, the balls, the *cojones* to be the success you are today? You and Celeste are exactly alike. Don't do this to her." "Get out before I call the authorities," she said. "You know, I hate to bring this up, Barbara, but you still owe me vacation pay," I could feel the sweat trickling down my armpits. "You never paid me that $1,500 dollars as stipulated in our contract, and now you've destroyed my $500.00 phone. I'll leave quietly if you cut me a check for $2,000 dollars. A winner like you ought to do the right thing." She grabbed a half-filled wine glass from the mantle and smashed it against the wall. She stared at me for a few moments. I stared back, "You like to smash things, don't you, Barbara?" I asked. As she walked toward me I backed up, turned around, and left down the stairs. But on the way out I stopped and grabbed several valuable trinkets and statuettes, slipping them into my book bag. I just took them, ya know what I'm saying? I took them because I am a winner. I am the definition of success. I am self-made. That is who I am.

The goodies were later appraised at a total value of $4,000. Considering I was still out $500.00 for my phone and $1,500 in unpaid salary, I wasn't really as big of a winner and I would have liked to have been.

As I walked out the front door onto the walkway, I

turned around and looked back at the mansion. I saw Barbara staring out the window at me from the third floor with a drink in her hand, and from the second floor I saw Celeste staring out the window. But she wasn't looking at me and she didn't wave or jump up and down and shout or blow me a kiss like she normally did. She was just staring straight ahead. I waved at her but she didn't wave back.

The Sluts of Saturn

in this savage age twisted by historians
we have flung our names to Wall Street.
tortured with a mouth full of words
not one shred of love or courage can slip through.
release this hunger
that unfolds the depths of oceans in your eyes
the universe slapping its pages
understands more than the pits and scars
of those who murder under the moonlit waltz of violins
of those who murder by annihilation with realigned teeth
and political correctness
of those who murder with creative marketing strategies and
authentic, organic crises
of those who murder simply by rolling over in their sleep.

kiss my eyes
kiss my lips
kiss my hair
It was a thought I had once before the winter frost
overtook me
before the fisherman hooked my pretty red heart
and splashed its guts on the deck
before the buses zoomed down Pico Boulevard
leaving me choking in the wake.

I am I think I was because I take no comfort
at a rocket wedged between two countries
burning on crosses that stretch toward the August sky.

all of my friends are ranting on Facebook
they are dying with each selfie
they are diminished with each status update
they are fed on newsfeed
and they like the like that likes the like
and it is *like*
a gutless and boundless deep space
where everyone is made of stars
that twinkle like glitter on a birthday card
but nobody is celebrating anything.
a photo of her discarded underpants feeds into a quiche
in the shape of a vagina, which bleeds into
a beheading in Syria,
that leads to a Buddhist incantation and self immolation,
which streams the Beach Boys, help me Rhonda, help me
Rhonda, help me Rhonda.

I don't know who my friends are
I can't identify my enemies
and it is a torment this waiting beyond weeping or grief
that perplexes me into octagons of dreaming and surrender
it is death made easy by the security cameras
it is death made easy by information overload
it is death made easy by the giddiness of the commentators
those sluts of Saturn who will wink at any sweet meat
who flashes their quivering quim at the slobbering bulldog
in the goo pot where the fur back turtle
with the rusty axe wound
waits in the dead end street.

I lay down my hands in retreat
I unscrew my head and all the bluebirds fly out
no one is coming
no one is watching.

The Whale Watchers

The three men set out from San Pedro Harbor at 8 a.m. in a small motor boat, armed with a cooler full of beer and sandwiches. All three had Tuesday off from their production jobs in Hollywood. Danny took the helm, putting on his Dodger's baseball cap, his iPod blasting Jimi Hendrix , while Hank snapped photographs of the U.S.S. Iowa and various cargo ships docked along the port. Steve was already drinking a beer and Danny (steering the wheel with his elbows) was rolling a joint that he planned on smoking once they got out of the harbor and into prime whale watching territory. "This is the life, man. This is the fuckin' life," Steve said as he lay back in his seat, adjusting his sun visor, his right hand skimming the water. He reached for the can in his drink caddy and chugged it down. "So, what happened last week?" Hank asked Steve. "We saw two Grays just off Portuguese Bend," Hank said, still snapping shots of the harbor boats. "Fuck! I wish I hadn't missed that," Steve said, throwing back his brew. "Last week I was stuck with another director who thinks he's Stanley Kubrick. Forty takes to get a couple of dumb models to step out of a car in front of a green screen."

Steve pulled out a pair of binoculars, studying a flock of seagulls on the horizon. "Those Honda people really opened their wallets for this one. Golden hours but it knocked me on my ass," Steve said. Finishing his beer, he let out a belch, and grabbed another can from the ice chest. "That's the last time I'm ever dealing with *that* shit again," Steve sighed and chugged down more of his beer." "Sucks, man, but the money's worth it." Danny said, putting his joint kit away. "No," Steve said. "It's not worth it anymore." Steve slouched down in his seat looking off into the distance. The binoculars hung from his neck. Danny, spotting Hank's plumber's ass, grabbed his Smartphone and took a shot of Hank bending over to get a photo of a tug boat. "Dude," Danny called out to Hank, "I just sent a shot of your ass to Marie!" Without turning around, Hank gave Danny the finger. Danny snapped a shot of that too.

They slowly made their way out of the harbor. Hours passed while Hank took photos of boats and marine life. Danny stayed at the helm blasting Otis Redding and Cream from his iPod. Steve was quiet as he drank one beer after another. Danny fired up the weed, handing joints to Hank and Steve. Steve smiled, inhaling deeply. He let the smoke linger in his lungs for as long as he could before exhaling and then taking another long, deep drag. He played air guitar during a rift in Cream's Strange Brew. Danny picked up an imaginary guitar and joined in for a few moments but then cut the music as they approached a buoy with several sea lions sunning themselves. The baby sea lions had flopped on the backs and bellies of their mothers and fathers in a blubbery, drunken sleep, their wet skins glistening in the sun. Two adult males were hoisting themselves up on their front fins eyeing the boat. Hank focused the camera in on the babies and managed to get several expert shots. Danny maneuvered the boat so that they continuously circled the buoy at a fifty-foot radius for the next five minutes. Steve inhaled the aroma of the sea lions. They smelled of fish, sea weed, and salt. He noticed the way one of the mothers had her left front fin protectively around her cub. He looked at all the cubs as they slept, their twitching whiskers, their tiny fins, the way their half sleeping mothers caressed them with their noses. "I had a dog once. Looked just like that. A really great dog." Just then, one of the slumbering pups woke up and looked at Steve with drowsy eyes. He barked several times as he slid off of his mother's back, waddled to the edge of the buoy, and dove into the ocean. The father sea lion followed him. Hank and Danny hadn't noticed that Steve had started to cry. When they finally did notice they looked at each other then looked away. They both thought the moment would quickly pass but it didn't. Danny, confused, navigated away from the buoy. Hank, smiling, sat down next to Steve and said, "Hey, buddy, you okay?" He reached into the cooler and pulled out a sandwich. "Why don't you go a little easy on the weed and sop up some of the suds with this?" Steve put his joint down, took the sandwich and started eating it. "Hank, you ever wonder why we spend most of our time doing things we don't wanna to do? I never thought about it until a few months ago. But now it just eats at me all the time." Hank looked at

Steve as he reached into his bag, pulled out a water bottle with some pink liquid in it and took a sip. "This is for my ulcer," he said, belching. "Jesus, it tastes like shit." He had stopped crying by then. " Ya know, you guys, it would be epic to see some whales, or even a pod of dolphins," Steve said, chomping on his sandwich to get the chalky aftertaste out of his mouth. No more than five minutes had passed when Hank saw a dozen fins break the surface of the water. He motioned for Danny to cut the motor. He turned around to Steve and said, "Look Stevo, dolphins!" There were a hundred dolphins surrounding the boat. Steve threw his sandwich down, grabbed the bottle of pink liquid and downed it. He climbed to the bow of The Boston Whaler. Peering over the handrail, he let out a yelp as the dolphins swam in front of the boat. Some of them sprang out of the water. Steve yelped again when he saw the leaping dolphins. "This is the greatest, you guys! This is fuckin' awesome!" He ripped off his shorts, underwear, and t-shirt. He threw his shoes, socks, visor, and binoculars on the deck and jumped into the ocean.

Hank and Danny looked at each other and ran to the side of the boat, staring at Steve swimming nude with the dolphins. "Steve," Hank screamed, "What the hell are ya doing?" Steve kept repeating, "I'm free. I'm free. I'm free." Hank and Danny looked at each other again, "Look buddy, we know you've been going through some shit," Hank screamed to Steve, "Grab my hand. C'mon now." Hank had his hand extended toward Steve, but Steve kept swimming further out into the ocean. Danny, back at the helm, started the motor up again and followed Steve as he swam with the dolphins. Hank and Danny smiled nervously at each other, shrugging their shoulders, staring at Steve. After a few minutes, Hank called out to Steve, "Stevo, time to come in now buddy." "No! I'm staying out here," Steve said. "Hank, get your camera. I have something to say." "What the hell is this all about, Steve?" Hank screamed. "Get your ass back in the boat right now. You're drunk and you're high." "I'll get back in the boat if you could just film the speech I want to make. It won't take long. Get your camera, Hank. I'll wait." Hank picked up his camera, switched it to video, and as instructed began filming Steve. "To whom it may concern," Steve said, looking directly into the lens. "I drank a cocktail of oxy and sleeping pills a few minutes ago, enough to kill three horses. I'll be gone soon. I want to die today with the dolphins in the ocean. These two guys are my best friends," he pointed to Hank and Danny, whose mouths had fallen open at the same time. "They have nothing to do with this. It's all my idea. I have pancreatic cancer and I've only got about six months left anyway. Six months of shit." Hank put the camera down while it was still rolling and both men extended their hands to Steve, shouting at him to get the fuck back on board. Danny threw him a life preserver. Steve picked it up and flung it away from him. Danny, looking at Hank said, "Hank, get over here and hold the wheel." Hank who had picked up his camera again, managed to keep the camera rolling with one hand while grabbing the wheel with the other. Danny had already jumped into the ocean and was swimming toward Steve. "Is it true Steve? What you said?

Is it true?" Danny asked, out of breath. "Yes, it's true." The two men looked at each other. "It's cold out here. Come back on the boat." "No. This is the way I want to go. Swimming with the dolphins. Maybe finding a Gray." "Is there anything I can do for you?" "Nothing. Just let me go," Steve said. "C'mon, man. Get back up on deck. We can come up with a better solution to this uh, this, you know, this predicament." Steve let out a laugh. He threw his hands up in the air. They landed back down in the water with a splash. "Predicament? This is not a little predicament. I'm dying, goddamn it. I'm gonna be dead in six months. I'm not getting back up on deck. Why should I? So I can work myself to death for a little bit longer? For what? For my stupid job? And for a woman who doesn't respect me? Is that how we die?" The three men stared at each other for several moments. "What was any of it ever for? What the fuck was any of it ever for?" Steve shouted to Hank and Danny. Hank and Danny looked at each other. Hank let out a heavy sigh, shaking his head, "It's what we do, Steve." "Well, it's not what I do anymore. I am now a free man!" Steve shouted, smiling. He turned around and dove into the ocean. Hank and Danny could see his bare behind just before it became submerged by the dark water. They stared at the bubbles that surfaced as he swam several feet away from the boat. When he came up for air he said, "Hank, I'm gonna finish up here! Put your goddamned camera on me" Hank picked up his camera and looked at Steve. "What are ya waitin' for motherfucker? Put your goddamned camera on me now!" Hank put his eye up to the camera lens and focused in on Steve. "There is a sealed envelope to my lawyer in my safe deposit box at the bank." Steve swam closer to the camera. "Fuck you, Carol. You soul-sucking leech. I supported you for thirty years and all you do is go on Facebook and Twitter and bitch about how stupid men are with all your feminist pals who are also living off their husbands. Well, you'll soon be doing a new dance, honey. It's called WORKING. The gravy train has stopped, baby. Consider yourself liberated! And by the way, I know all about that asshole pool man." Steve splashed sea water on his face and stared into the camera one last time, letting out a measured **F-U-C-K Y-O-U!**

Steve looked at Hank and Danny. Danny extended his hand to Steve. Steve, smiling, nodded his head, no. "Listen, you two assholes have been my only real friends for the past twenty-five years." he said, smiling at Hank and Danny. "You're the only ones I give a shit about." Steve looked at his friends one last time. He then focused his gaze at the ocean's distant horizon. "I'm sorry to put this on you," Steve shook his head. Hank and Danny looked at each other again and then at Steve. "Danny, crank up Hendrix," Steve said. "You know the song I wanna hear." Danny found the song he knew Steve loved the most and blasted it from the small boat. Steve sang the words, "Purple haze all in my brain. Lately things don't seem the same. Actin' funny but I don't know why. 'Scuse me while I kiss the sky." He threw his head back and howled in the air. "Now I'm gonna go find me some of those Gray's," he slurred. Steve felt his muscles relax. He let the current carry him away from the boat. Smiling, he gave a slow wave to

Hank and Danny, who only half raised their hands to him, while Hendrix belted out, "You got me blowin' blowin' my mind. Is it tomorrow or the end of time?" He turned around and swam further and further out into the ocean. Hank and Danny watched their friend swim away from them until he was barely a dot on the surface of the sea.

Hank turned off the camera and put it down, unable to speak. Danny turned the Boston Whaler around and headed back to the port. Both men were silent as they cracked open fresh beers and ate their sandwiches. Afterward, they each lit up a joint. They leaned back in their seats with their sunglasses on, taking their hats and shirts off to let the afternoon sun shine on their faces and warm their bodies. They inhaled the marine air and watched the seagulls flying above them. In the distance they heard the bark of sea lions on a buoy. They had never felt more alive.

Edendale

It's been years since I've lived in Echo Park. I lived there before the dilapidated boathouse was refurbished and the lake dredged. Before the homeless were kicked out of the park. Before they put an end to the food vendors that filled the lake grounds on the weekends. Before the guns, shopping cart, telephone booth, and wagon wheel were found in the layers of mud under the lake. The wagon wheel was from one of the surrounding ranches from the 1800's that no longer exist. Every morning I'd walk around the lake three times, pulling birdseed out of my pockets and throwing it into the air. But sometimes I had to be careful about feeding the birds because they would surround me with their sheer numbers. When I ran out of food I'd start to back away from the flock but they would swarm in on me, some pecking at my flesh and jabbing at my eyes. I'd walk home on Sunset Boulevard through two crumbling sandstone cliffs called "The Cut." It always made me think of the land being blasted and chiseled to build the railroad route that once took customers from downtown Los Angeles to an ostrich farm in Griffith Park.

Sometimes when I'd walk the streets of Echo Park I could feel the forces that wanted to claim the land. It wasn't just the moneyed people driven by greed and investments that had made their way in. The gangs that were already there would leave their hieroglyphics on the hundred-year-old walls around the houses of the neighborhood. Coyotes, raccoons, opossums, and the occasional mountain lion lurked in the hills and in our backyards at night. The incantations of the lunatic gospel of Aimee Semple McPherson preaching salvation still whispered from the Angelus Temple. And everywhere there were signs that Scientology was steadily oozing into every crevice of Los Angeles. There was an earthquake one day while I was in La Guadalupana Market. Groceries flew off the shelves and landed with a crash on the floor. Mothers pushing strollers, trailed by screaming children ran out into the street in a panic. There was also a series of fires that burned in the hills for several days, and from my room I watched them with binoculars. The cinders fell from the sky like snowflakes in the 101-degree weather.

Los Angeles is a city with amnesia. I had been one of those Angelinos who didn't know or care what came before them. But Echo Park awakened something in me. I started to pay attention to my city. I would walk through the historic district of Angelino Heights and when I'd come upon a particularly spectacular Victorian house I would jot down the address and look up the history of it on my computer when I got home. I found out where Buster Keaton, Fatty Arbuckle, The Three Stooges, Laurel and

Hardy, and Chaplin filmed their silent movies, and where one of Mack Sennett's studios had been. I became enamored of the rich history of the area; Hispanics comprising the majority of the population, Asians, Whites, and Blacks following them. Like most free-lance writers, my life was centered around going to the mailbox and looking for a check. So when a national magazine finally called me back and gave me the green light to go ahead and write an article I had pitched to them about the history of Echo Park, I was elated. I cranked up the music on my stereo and jumped up and down in the air, dancing around my room. Constantly short of money, I wanted to collect the $2,000 check they were to pay me, as soon as possible, so I told them I would have the article finished in five days. I worked at a brisk pace the first two days, but I realized that I needed to take a different approach if I was to make the article stand out. There was something missing from the story, but I hadn't quite figured out just what that was yet.

I lived in a carriage house behind my landlady's old Victorian on Kellam Avenue. A registered historical monument, it was built in 1880 to house horses and carriages during the pre-auto era. Though it was renovated, it had no heating system or air conditioner. During the summer the temperature inside my room could rise to 108 degrees. I dubbed it "The Elegant Inferno."

It was during a heat wave on the day before my article was due that I went to a party on Carroll Avenue. I had been sitting at the counter at The Brite Spot eating a vegetable omelet when a girl next to me asked me if I wanted to go to a party that afternoon. I almost said no, but then I thought, why not? I can't just stay inside the house and write every waking hour. I've got to get out once in awhile. But as soon as I got there I started to think it was a mistake. Not knowing anyone and being an essentially shy person made me feel awkward and out of my element. So I busied myself consuming a bowl of spinach dip and three beers. The girl from The Brite Spot brushed by me and said, "Hey, I'm glad you made it! Easy on that dip though, it's potent!" I heard her giggling as she rejoined her group. I was starting to feel a little light-headed. I looked around at some of the partygoers. They were an organic group of vegan groovsters who had embraced a seventies retro look. Some were smoking weed, others were hanging out by the BBQ, and others were going skinny-dipping in the pool. I grabbed another beer and ate some more of the spinach dip. My head was really starting to swirl when I heard a girl say, "Hey, I have an idea. Let's ALL take our clothes off! Come on, let's get NAKED!" I watched her undo her bra and let her breasts bounce out. She took her tie-dye skirt off. She was not wearing underwear. Her full black bush was the major attraction of the group at that moment. I saw it grow at least a foot until it looked like she was sporting an enormous Afro on her crotch. Then two nude men come up behind her. They started to engage in a threesome. I'm not a prude or anything, but the whole scene was happening way too fast, and my head was spinning, and I had an article due the next day. A guy dressed in a train conductor uniform came up to me and told me that if I didn't take my clothes off at the next stop he'd write me up a citation. I mumbled that I had to go home and left the party on horseback. I turned around before I left and saw about three hundred naked people engaged in sex acts. Some of them were up in the trees, on the fence, and on the roof.

It was only a five-block walk back to the carriage house. On the way home I had the horse take a dirt trail that followed a stream where native women were dipping jugs into the water and carrying them on their heads. Children were bathing in the stream, splashing and laughing. I wanted to join them, but there was a saber-toothed tiger stalking me (its incisors were a foot long) so I galloped at full speed all the way home. When I opened the door of the carriage house the hot air smelled of hay. I could hear the neigh of horses and their hooves clomping on the wooden floorboards. I tied my horse to the post. I heard the hammering of horseshoes and heavy work boots walking toward me. A male voice spoke to the horses, but I looked around and nobody was there. I went upstairs, turned on all the fans, opened the windows, and turned on the computer to finish my article. I sat there feeling the room sway as if I were being rocked by waves in the ocean. I looked at my hands. They were turning into bird claws. I looked in the mirror. I had transformed into an eagle. I felt myself flying around the room. I could see my wings flapping. I looked down at my bed from the ceiling and I saw how small I was sitting at my desk typing at my computer. I was only a tiny dot. A voice spoke to me. It told me to escape from Echo Park. I flew out the hay door and soared above the houses and the hills. I passed over Echo Park Lake, swooped down, and grabbed a rattlesnake in my talon. I ripped its head off with my beak and ate it. I headed toward the La Brea Tar Pits, making a crash landing in the marsh. I smelled the methane gas and felt myself being dragged under the bubbling crude oil. I was dragged through layers of primordial muck going back to the ice age. I surfaced in a vat of moonshine in an underground speakeasy in downtown Los Angeles. Drunk from the liquor, I flew through a series of subterranean tunnels, banging my head several times until I found a portal to the sky. It was the bluest sky I had ever seen. In the distance I saw acres and acres of orange trees and strawberry fields. I flew up past the clouds beyond Earth's atmosphere and looked down at Echo Park, and saw miles of lush, green land and reservoirs. I flew up higher into space. There were stars twinkling in the darkness as far as the eye could see. Up ahead a gigantic neon billboard flashed the name, EDENDALE. It promised pure air and a temperate, healthful climate. Colossal houses rose from the nearby stars like cathedrals. A separate planet was covered with crops, livestock, and massive bodies of water. A family was floating in the darkness, holding hands, and looking wistfully off into the solar system.

PLANETS

so removed were my feelings for them
that by the time my Dad had a coronary
and my Mom drove the station wagon into
the side of the mountain,
I took it as a good sign.
the house took on a new dimension
with those two out of the picture.
I took to having TV dinners every night
in front of the tube
where I learned to appreciate
the beauty of baseball-
all that grace in one slow-motion playback
made my face glow like a moon baby,
and one night I saw a movie about a killer,
he held a knife to a boy's chest
as if to slice a tender piece of pink ham,
but thinking twice, threw the knife in the earth
and let the boy run home to his mother.
I had never thought about baseball
or second chances.
I had never considered that the
ghastly light which filters through a screen
is as real as a player clutching his heart
on a baseball field
where small planets are being sent out
like radar, rebounding off the sides
of mountains, orbiting around some woman's head,
fanatical in their search for a home

away from home,
ending up at a drunken brawl.
yet I see them, time and time again,
catch each other in each other's hands
and run straight back to home base,
and I hear them say, "well Martha, another game won."

how a heart knows when to stop
is beyond me.
and now
as light filters through the screen
I sit in front of the tube
with all my senses intact.

Pepper

It may have been the heat wave, or it could have been the fact that I was renting a room from a certifiably insane woman. Maybe it was those twelve hour shifts I put in at Cathleen's Restaurant after one of the waitresses, Amber, had an epiphany early Sunday morning in the kitchen. She had four plates stacked on her left arm and three plates weighing on her right arm. Looking directly at Cathleen, her glossy pink mouth issued a statement, "Kiss my fuckin' ass you dried up old hag!" There was a crashing of plates after she threw both arms down and without missing a beat simultaneously raised the middle finger on each hand. "I am so outta here!" she screamed as she ripped off her polyester burgundy apron and threw it on the floor. Looking directly at Cathleen she said, "keep my tips, bitch, you need them more than I do."

None of us knew exactly what had happened between Amber and Cathleen. Amber was considered to be the free spirit of the restaurant. Amber, it was thought by some of the waitresses, had too much self-esteem to be working for someone as domineering and controlling as Cathleen. Well, maybe that was true about Amber, I thought. But I didn't have time to think about self-esteem. I just needed more money so I could move the hell away from my crazy landlady. Right after Amber walked out the back door still cursing and waving her arms with the exhilaration of her new found emancipation, I walked over to Cathleen and told her that I would cover all of Amber's shifts.

It seemed like a good idea at the time, but as I walked to the bus stop on Colorado Boulevard in the 102 degree Pasadena heat, I realized I had worked double shifts every day for the past week. I felt edgy as I walked down the sidewalk past the elegant homes and lush gardens. I was annoyed that I was starting to perspire, since I had taken special care with applying my makeup that morning. The better I look, the more money I'll make, I reasoned. But how am I supposed to look attractive in this kind of heat? I sat down on a bus bench that was mercifully located under the shade of a giant oak tree. I took out my compact and dabbed at the perspiration on my upper lip. A man swinging a silver chain walked by. He turned around, "Hey Baby, ya got any change?" He asked. "Yes, I have change," I held up a roll of quarters. "It's for the bus, not you." "Well, I was just wonderin' if you might have somethin' extra," he said smiling and winking at me. "Extra?" I laughed. "I'm sorry, I'm afraid I don't understand the concept. I've got some money but none of it is *extra*, alright?" He walked closer to me. "Say, what's a nice lookin' well-to-do lady like yourself taking the bus for?" He grinned, flashing his smile. "Mmmmmmmm," he said, edging closer to me. "I like that short hair on a woman.

That is STYLISH! You French or somethin'?" I pulled out my pepper spray and positioned it toward him. "Oh lady," he laughed. "That stuff stings." He looked at me perplexed, "You don't like brothers?" he asked, frowning. "I have a brother," I said, "You're not him." I looked at him more closely. "You don't even remember me, do you?" I asked. He grinned, "Sure, I remember you, baby, sure." I remembered his smile from two days ago when I was waiting at another bus stop a few miles away. I had reached into my pocket, taken out a five, and handed it to him. "Let me clue you in," I grabbed the hideous floral tie I was wearing. "Does this look rich to you?" I held up the polyester burgundy apron with my name tag on it and shoved it in his face. "Does this speak of wealth?" His mouth dropped open. "You know, this is the second time you've asked me for money this week. What do I look like to you? Bank of America?" I got up off the bench and faced him. "No, really, I want to know what you see when you look at me." I grabbed the silver chain that was secured to his jeans and gave it a yank. I could smell the beer on his breath. "What do you think a bitch like me is supposed to do when they are approached by a guy like you begging for money?" He laughed, shaking his head, "Now, now, laydee, let's just be nice. Let's keep it nice." "Should I go ahead and give you all my cash, strip nude, and spread for you right here at the bus stop?" I yanked on his chain harder this time. He looked disturbed as he backed away from me, grabbing the chain from my hand. "Oh lady, c'mon," he said, shaking his head and holding up his hands. "This is crazy talk." "Crazy?" I asked, moving even closer to him.

"Gimme a break, lady," he said, backing up again and walking away. "Break?" I laughed. I ran out in front of him, "There is no break!" I shrieked in his face. "There is never going to be a break!" I pressed the button of the pepper spray, missing him entirely. "Jesus Christ!" He screamed, covering his eyes and nose, turning around, and running away. "Crazy ass broad! I never know what kinda freaks I'm gonna find out here!"

The bus approached as he fled. Its doors opened in front of me. I walked up the stairs, put my fare into the machine, said hello to the bus driver, and took a seat. The air was crisp and cool, a welcome change. Why was I so hard on that guy? Am I crazy like he said? Just then I saw him walking along the street. I waved to him, smiling. As the bus passed him, I turned around and saw him shouting something. He flipped me the bird, holding it until I was two blocks down the boulevard and out of his view. Well, maybe I am crazy. But then again, maybe it's just the heat, I thought as the bus turned the corner and zoomed up Lake Avenue toward Cathleen's Restaurant.

Hancock Park

Although I had only lived in Hancock Park a few months, I came to feel as if I had lived there my entire life. I enjoyed walking through the neighborhood at night because I could see inside the well-lit mansions and imagine myself living in grandeur. I had imagined a life without poverty before, but this was different. Besides I wasn't quite as poor as I used to be. After four years of being a personal assistant to a Hollywood producer, I had amassed a savings that, modest though it was, made me feel powerful. Instead of the old nightmares that used to paralyze me in my sleep, I started to have dreams, or perhaps delusions of great wealth and prestige. I can't place where I was in these dreams. Actually, it wasn't a particular place I was in but rather a state of being. It was a new kind of hunger that replaced the old hunger I used to have for food. I never forgot the times when I hadn't had enough to eat. I would go to work in the morning with hunger pangs and by noon be light headed with the familiar gnawing and growling in my stomach. I'd have a peanut butter sandwich and an apple for lunch, and by five be ravenous again. That was the old hunger, but what surprised me about the new hunger was that it seemed to originate from the same place the old hunger did: my gut. It came directly from my gut, and it drove me like an animal.

On my nightly constitutionals I studied the people who lived in the splendid old mansions of Hancock Park. Sometimes I would stop in front of someone's living room window and watch them while they argued with their spouse, or sat in their easy chair, watching television alone in the dark with a glass of bourbon in their hand. Sometimes I would get so close to the open window that I could hear the ice clinking in their drink, and smell the pot roast wafting through the air. I would often have to position myself behind trees or hedges so as not to be detected. One night I heard a woman crying in the shower. From the sidewalk I could smell her soap. It was pure castile with a hint of peppermint. I looked up at her bathroom window, listening to her sob and curse. She let out a low guttural moan that had a rhythm and cadence all its own. She was still moaning after she turned off the water. Then I heard a great crash and shattering of glass. She must have smashed the bathroom mirror, which made her cry even louder. Another family I studied were perpetually on their iPhones and other electronic devices. I watched them with binoculars from behind the Jacaranda in their front yard. They were served dinner by hired help in their dinning room every night. They ate from china and drank from crystal, but they were each trapped in their own cyber world. They laughed at what they saw on Facebook,

Twitter, and Instagram, and chatted using Bluetooth, but I never saw them speak to or even look at one another.

There was a young man, a little older than me, twenty-five or twenty-six, whose cat would sit on top of his Steinway while he played concertos. The way he played Bach, Mozart, and Beethoven made the cravings in my belly grow stronger. One night he caught me listening to him playing Bach but luckily he had a sense of humor. He stood up from his piano, stuck his head out the window and said, "You are either a criminal and I should call the police, or you're a secret admirer and I should invite you in for tea." I stepped away from the hedge I was hiding behind, "I'm sorry," I said, tripping as I walked out into the flood of light in front of his living room window, "I'm not a criminal. I was just enjoying your playing. I'm going now." I heard him laugh as I walked away, "Do you live in the neighborhood?" he called out. I just kept walking. "I'll see you around, neighbor!" He waved at me, smiling, as if it were the most normal thing in the world to find a peeping Tom on his lawn.

Not all my neighbors lived in mansions. I lived in a one-room apartment on Mansfield. There were several places like mine on my street. They were built in the 1920's. My apartment had been in my landlady's family for seventy-five years. So had the apartment next to me which she had been living in most of her life. One night I was arranging my belongings in the closet. Struggling to get the bottom cedar drawer to close, I pulled it out and put it back on its tracks.

But it still refused to close all the way. So I took the drawer out again, got down on the floor, reached my arm all the way back in, and felt what I thought was a paperback book. I grabbed it and saw that it was really a stack of photographs tied together with string. I untied the string and laid the photos out on my kitchen table, brushing the dust off of them with a dish towel. There were about a hundred photographs of people from the '30's and '40's taken all over Hancock Park. One of the pictures was of a pensive young woman in a black dress and black gloves, holding a bouquet of lilies, looking out the living room window of my apartment. I turned the photo over and in ballpoint pen it said, " April 4th, 1942." I could see a resemblance to that of my landlady. They were her family photographs.

As I looked at the photos I wondered what it was like to be a part of a family. What was it like to look like someone else, to have the same nose, eyes, and hair? Was it comforting to share their history or was it a trap? I wondered if their roots bound them together in family unity or if they constricted the flow of blood to their veins until they were lifeless. I took several of the photographs and propped them up around my apartment so that their faces were watching me as I sat in the middle of my living room. As I looked into their eyes it seemed that some of them started to look at me accusingly, bitterly. They blamed me for their half-lived, disappointed lives. Others were laughing at me and making remarks about my "nighttime shenanigans and tomfoolery," as they put it. They were telling me to grow up and face "the way life really is."

I fell asleep that night dreaming that I was lying in a dirt pit looking up at the moon and the stars. I could see the walls of the pit and I could hear people moaning. They were moaning and crying, and I could feel them writhing underneath me. I was in a mass grave of wounded and dead people. In the moonlight I could see my dress drenched in their blood. My only thought was to get out alive. I got up and walked over their bodies to the side of the pit. I stacked some of the dead in a mound, hoisted myself up by grabbing onto their limbs, and climbed out of the mouth of the pit. I ran toward the music I heard in the distance. It led me to a place that rose above the Hollywood Freeway. I was blinded by flood lights until the young man from Hancock Park who played the piano emerged from behind a tree into a grassy clearing. He took his place at the Steinway. His cat rolled over, lapping at the fur on his paws while he played Mozart's Piano Concerto Number 20 in D Minor. "I'm glad you figured it out, neighbor," he said. "Figured what out?" I asked. He smiled at me and continued to play.

Girlie Show

It's the spotlight glaring in my eyes
that saves me the sight of anyone's face.
While striding the stage I tear off my dress
and it flies up behind me like a pair of wings.
I imagine I'm strutting the roof of a high-rise
and when I look down I see
the rats and roaches crawling the surface of the earth,
I look up and I am blinded by the sun.

But I must tread the edge of the skyscraper in stiletto heels,
naked,
my wings spread behind me,
the music blaring,
lifting me above the laughter of the hyenas
as they feed, and drink,
and watch.

Chapel on Wheels

When he was a child he'd watch old westerns on Sunday mornings in his pajamas, while eating a bowl of corn flakes. He'd wake up at 7 am, grab his cowboy hat, put his cowboy boots on, and sit in front of the television set watching cowboys in shootouts and stampedes. At night he dreamt of galloping on the vast plains and deserts of the West. He could feel his body and the body of the horse he was riding become a single body that galloped as fast as it could and steered itself to uncharted territories. Sometimes he would wake up with a jerk when he dreamt that his horse lost its footing in the high chaparral. He often didn't know if he was falling to the ground or falling into outer space. Sometimes he dreamt of floating in a terrain that was half Wild West and half deep space.

He loved going horseback riding and camping outdoors on the weekends. He and his father would ride their horses into the woods, stake out a site and build a fire at night to keep warm. They would heat up a can of baked beans and brew coffee on the open flame. They roasted sausages with tree branches his father sharpened into spears. Sometimes they would fish in the lake and have trout for dinner. As they toasted their marshmallows on the fire, the boy and his father made up fantastical stories about how the earth and the animals first came into being. Together they created their own mythology about the origins of Earth and the Milky Way. The boy's father always brought his guitar and harmonica with him and would sing old cowboy songs to the boy. These songs were often about the death of a cowboy. But death, even if it was death by hanging, was always faced with bravery and honor. Sometimes the songs would evoke in the boy a sense that he was making magical discoveries about the world. He would look up into the night sky and wonder where it ended. It had to end somewhere, he thought. His father tried to explain infinity to him, but he wasn't much good at it. The boy asked his father if he could have a telescope for his 10th birthday that was coming up in a few weeks. The father looked at his son from across the fire. He understood the boy's curiosity, and he hoped the boy would not settle, as he had, on a life that was limited and tame. The father worked for the state road maintenance crew. Daily, he repaired potholes in the very roads he longed to be driving away on.

It was a family ritual for the boy, his father, and mother to go to the local movie theater every Friday night. Built in 1923, The Rialto was an old-fashioned one room theater with red velvet drapes and ornate wood work on the ceiling and walls. The ticket takers were dressed in the same type of uniform that their predecessors wore eighty-five years ago. In the darkness of the theater the boy would lose himself much in the same way he lost himself sitting around the campfire telling stories and listening to his father sing. With each new story projected onto the screen the boy saw in himself the promise of a new adventure and a different way of travelling   through the world.

When the boy was old enough for Junior High School he stopped going to the theater with his parents and started going with his buddies instead. But his friends only wanted to see the most inane blockbusters of the type that didn't interest the boy. Sometimes he would go to the theater by himself and watch the movies that spoke to him. In daydreams he often saw himself on a vast battlefield marching with the other soldiers through bombed out cities that he had seen in movies. At times he found himself in a jungle hacking through vegetation with a machete, discovering the ruins of an extinct civilization. Other times he saw himself starring in silent movies. In the corner of the stage a hunched over piano player banged out tunes as the boy was blown up with dynamite, run over by a train, sawed in half, and hung by the neck until dead. And at other times when he was alone in his room staring at the blank white wall he imagined himself in a sort of nowhere land that seemed to stretch on forever. It was as if he lived on an empty plain that could tilt and bend and go on for eternity.

As the boy got older he found it impossible to sit still in the classroom. He was a bright, articulate boy but he had been in the grip of wanderlust for years. Although he had been enjoying working on his father's friend's ranch every weekend for five years, he knew it was time to make his own way. And one night he packed his bags and left at two in the morning. He didn't want to tell his parents he was leaving. He knew his mother would try to keep him in high school. He knew his father would want him to go out into the world, but would hold him back, out of fear mostly. So he took a bus out of town, then took another bus to Colorado. His plan was to work with horses at a ranch by day, and sit out by the campfire at night, cooking his dinner and studying the stars with his telescope. When he got to Colorado he headed straight to the nearest ranch and talked to the owner. The owner liked the boy's enthusiasm and could see that he had done the work he claimed. By that time the boy had grown tall and robust. His dark hair fell in his face when he laughed, which was often. His olive skin was made darker by days spent in the sun working horses. The owner didn't feel the need to check the boy's work history. He put the boy to work the next day, and was pleased to find that he had been right about him. The boy was more than competent. He had a natural talent for handling horses. And his exuberance for hard work rubbed off on some of the other young ranch hands he had hired. There was only one time when the boy had trouble with one of the other hands. One day the boy caught the cowboy rummaging through his things in the bunk house that the ranch hands shared. He saw the cowboy slip the leather handled hunting knife that had once belonged to his grandfather in his jacket. The boy approached him and asked him for the knife back. When the cowboy denied that he had taken anything from the boy, the boy grabbed a broom, and in one lightening move, broke it in half by stomping on it with his foot, and shoving the splintered end to his throat. The boy held him there for several moments as a trickle of blood fell from the cowboy's throat where the jagged broom end had pierced his skin. "You wanna give me my knife back, fucker?" The boy said. The cowboy smiled. And in a raspy voice said, "I don't have your knife, asshole." The boy jammed the jagged broom a little further into his throat until he heaved, motioning with his hands that he was giving up. As the boy let him go, the cowboy reached into his jacket and pulled out the hunting knife, handing it to the boy. The other ranch hands respected the boy even more after seeing how he handled the thief. The boy never let on that he had seen a similar maneuver in a movie that he and his father had watched at The Rialto when he was eleven years old. The boy had been so impressed with the effectiveness of the maneuver that he went to the local five-and-dime and bought ten brooms with wooden handles. He took the brooms home and practiced breaking them with his foot and swinging the jagged end up into the throat of an imaginary adversary. After he performed the feat ten times he felt confident enough to add it to his growing repertoire of cinema stunts.

After a year at the ranch, it was clear to everyone that the boy was a natural born leader. The owner knew that the boy would not be satisfied with being a ranch hand much longer. And sure enough, after two years of working on the Colorado ranch, the boy decided to try his luck in another state. He had been corresponding with his parents, letting them know that he was happy and doing well. He told them that he felt the "itch" to move on. He was 19 by then. The road was calling him.

He ended up in Sacramento, California. He found himself short on money, and with nowhere to call home, he gravitated to a movie Cineplex where he watched five movies consecutively. When he was done watching movies he checked in to a Motel 6 and slept for fifteen hours. The next day the boy applied to a trucking company and was hired immediately. For the first six months, he was elated with his new life of handling a big rig. He was happy to be on the open road, constantly moving. He had a knack for forming an instant camaraderie among the other truckers at the rest stops and cafes. There was an ease and joy about the boy that drew people to him. But being a good looking boy, he had to be careful. One night at a truck stop in New Jersey, the boy was approached by an older man who opened the cab of his truck and motioned for the boy to come in with him. The boy shook his head, and said, "no." He continued to walk to his big rig in the dark, looking behind him several times. He felt that he was being followed and as he turned around again, the man punched him in the face. "Nobody tells me no," the man said. The boy grabbed the man, throwing him on the gravel. He kicked the man in the groin and stomach several times until the man was unconscious. He then walked to his truck, got in and drove down the highway. The boy was shook but he knew it would soon pass. He drove a hundred and fifty miles to another rest stop, wiped the blood off his boots, and slept for six hours before embracing the open road again.

He did not want to let this one relatively minor incident ruin the job for him, but the truth was that the trucker's life was gradually starting to wear him down. Sitting for long periods of time was not what he had dreamed for himself. And to make matters worse, he was constantly under electronic control. The trucking company installed a GPS tracking device in all of their trucks. They knew exactly where all of their truckers were at all times. They knew where a trucker was parked and for how long he was parked there. This made the boy depressed. Where was the freedom in digital surveillance, he wondered. And besides, he missed the nights spent out on the open range, listening to coyotes, telling stories, and cooking his dinner on an open fire. He missed being able to look at the stars with his telescope every night. He needed to work, but he didn't want to be a truck driver anymore. One of the truckers at a rest stop in Needles told him about a film production company that was hiring film crew laborers. He told him that there were also jobs for extras sometimes.

The boy was excited at the prospect of having a job that involved working on movie sets. He decided to quit his trucker job right then and there. Within a week he got a ride out to Hollywood and an interview at the studio. He had two hours to kill before the actual interview. It was too hot to wait at the local park, so he found a coffee shop and had some road food; a chili burger with cheese, onions, and home fries, washed down with strong black coffee. When he was finished he walked up Van Ness Avenue, passing an elementary school with a little trailer parked in front of it. "Chapel On Wheels" it said. He had missed the church services that he used to go to with his parents back home. It wasn't that he believed in God so much as he missed the ritual of prayer. When he prayed he felt almost as free as when he was out on the open range. He walked in the side door of the chapel trailer, removed his Stetson, and knelt down in front of the altar. He thought about the stars in the black sky and the fire and the coyotes. He thought about his father's baritone voice as he sang of death and bravery. He thought about his dream of falling into the Wild West and ranging into deep space. He thought about the new dream he had been having every night. It was a new dream but it seemed to be interwoven with all of his old dreams. The new dream was that he was being watched by thousands, perhaps millions of people as he wondered through cities, deserts, mountains, and space. It awoke in him the same feelings of wonderment that he experienced in front of the camp fire at night roasting sausages on a wooden spear, the stars stretching out into infinity above him. It was the same transportive feeling he had while sitting in the darkness of the theater watching movies at The Rialto with his parents. And it was reminiscent of the times he trained horses on the ranch in Colorado. As he prayed he could smell the sage that grew on the high planes. He could see the fields of yarrow and taste the wild strawberries he picked as a child. He saw the open road stretching out ahead of him. He saw the faces of his parents sitting in their living room. His father, staring straight ahead at the television set, tired from working sixteen-hour days. These were all of the things he prayed for as he knelt at the alter inside the Chapel On Wheels.

When he was finished praying he looked at his watch. He had fifteen minutes to walk five blocks to the studio for his interview. He looked up from the alter and out the window. There was an homeless man screaming at the traffic, pushing a shopping cart full of empty plastic soda bottles past the ticky tacky houses across the street. He got up off of his knees, wiped the sweat off his brow with a bandana, put his cowboy hat on, and walked out the door of the chapel into the glare of the hot, merciless day.

Gary and Ray

For thirty years I was glued to a plastic crucifix on the top of Ethel's T.V. set in a trailer park in El Monte. Bitch croaked about a month ago and I ended up on sale for five dollars at a junk shop off of Magnolia. Rubbing soldiers with an Elvis whiskey decanter is not how I had dreamed of spending my twilight years. Besides, every time I tried to talk to him he just stared off into space with that Elvis sneer. I thought he was a stuck- up little turd who thought he was too good to give me the time of day. But when he turned around to swat a fly buzzing behind his head, I could see the crack in his skull, which explained why he never spoke. After that I felt awful for ever having thought anything bad about him. Anyway, I had gotten real sick of having to hear Ethel's soap operas all the time after she got laid off from the plant. And when she finally got another job, as soon as she'd come home from work every night, she'd turn on American Idol, Dancing With The Stars, or The Home Shopping Network. There's so much desperation in those shows that sometimes it would make my stigmata bleed. And it was a big pain in the ass because Ethel would have all of her little friends over to her trailer so they could watch me bleed during The Bachelor. They would just sit there gawking at me and taking photos while my blood collected in an empty Hungry Man T.V. Dinner tray.

It was about a year ago that I lost my best friend, Ray. Ethel bought Ray after she saw The Story Of The Bible on The History Channel. Turns out that Jesus didn't have blue eyes and fair skin like me. He was brown-eyed and dark. So Ethel ordered an "Authentic Nazarene Jesus" from The Home Shopping Network. When Ethel took him out of the box I was impressed by his long white gown. It had intricate gold stitching and a gold belt. He was wearing sandals made out of real leather. Even his hair looked better than mine. I had strawberry blond hair that was thinning at my temples. My skin was grey from the residue of the smoke that Ethel blew at me while she watched television. My white robe had been stained by the wine Ethel had sloshed on me one night as she adjusted her T.V. set. She cackled as she ripped off my wet robe and replaced it with a floral nightie that she swiped from one of her baby dolls she collected. I felt like a slob next to the new guy who had skin that glowed, brown eyes that caught the light, and thick dark hair that fell to his shoulders. When he moved it was as if his feet were on fire. He came with a hand carved wooden cross that Ethel positioned him on next to me on the T.V. I was pretty leery of him at first. I mean I had already been living on Ethel's Sony Trinitron for fifteen years, so I wasn't exactly in the mood to share the spotlight with another Jesus. Much less one about a thousand times better looking than me. But nevertheless, I knew I had to get along with him if we were both to live atop Ethel's Sony, so I said, "Welcome to the trailer park, Jesus." He laughed, and told me his name was Ray. He asked me what my name was and I told him, "Jesus."

"Bullshit!" he laughed again. "You look like a Gary. I'm gonna call you Gary." He asked me what I did for fun. I told him the truth, "Nothing, Man. I just stand here and watch Ethel drink and smoke. I can see the reflection of the T.V. screen in the microwave in front of me, so sometimes I watch the shows, but I try not to because they make me bleed." He looked into my eyes and said, "Stick with me, brother. It's the only way we're gonna make it."

That night, after Ethel had passed out drunk, Ray jumped off his cross and leapt over the set to where she was reclining on her Lay-Z-Boy. He took her bottle of Scotch and drank a third of it. He lit up one of her Pall Malls and smoked it, flicking the ashes into her Stardust Casino ashtray. Then he jumped up to the knick-knack shelf and started ogling the water nymphs in their pool. Ethel had a set of ten porcelain nymphs in a glass bowl designed to look like a pond for bathing. She had filled the glass pond with tap water and had fresh cut lilies floating on the surface. She had arranged the naked nymphs in seductive poses. It had never occurred to me that I could move around Ethel's trailer after she passed out every night, but Ray took it as a given that we had free reign of the place. He got ahold of the remote and turned the channel to the adult station. "Come on, Gary. Get your goddamned ass off that T.V. Come on down here and live a little, motherfucker!"

Every night was a new adventure with Ray. Sometimes we'd sneak out of Ethel's trailer and lay on our backs on the grass and look up at the stars in the sky. Ray would talk about what he had read that day from the set of Britannica Encyclopedias that Ethel's husband had left on her shelf after he split with her. The Cretaceous-Tertiary extinction event was always on his mind. Ray would go on for hours about why the dinosaurs died out. After Ethel bought her first computer Ray would get on the web and spend hours in video chat rooms while Ethel was at work. Sometimes after Ethel fell asleep in her chair at night, Ray would turn the camera on her and live stream her snoring, farting, and talking in her sleep. I don't know how he managed it, but he was able to get ahold of Ethel's PIN number and purchase his own iPhone on the internet. He opened up a Facebook page from his phone. He had over 4,000 friends from all over the world. He loved to take selfies of us swimming and drinking beer in Ethel's fiberglass pool. Sometimes Ray would snag a joint from Ethel's neighbor and we'd float on the inner tube getting high and eating the Hamburger Helper from Ethel's refrigerator.

I had fourteen of the best years of my life with Ray. But one night, about a year ago Ethel came home from work shit-faced and grumbling about the extra charges on her credit card. Apparently she had caught on to Ray's activities. She picked him up and looked into his eyes, "You are the one who has been using my credit card, drinking my liquor, smoking my cigarettes, eating my food, and playing fast and loose with my nymphs. God only knows what else you're up to, you sonofabitch!" Ray roared his baritone laugh in Ethel's face. Ethel lost it. "You sound just like my ex-husband!" she screamed, hurling him against the wall, smashing him to bits. That night I never bled so hard in my life. And it wasn't just blood. I started crying all the time too. Of course Ethel had to put me on display for the whole park to see every time I bled and cried. I really despised her. So when the old biddy finally bit the dust, I was happy as hell. I don't think I'll ever find another friend like Ray. I think about him all the time. And when I see guys like Elvis next to me with the cracked skull and empty eyes, well, I just want to throw myself off the highest shelf of this junk store and feel myself smash into a thousand tiny pieces and have it done with for once and for all. It's a strange feeling to know that the best years of my life are already behind me.

Dinner at Denny's

I worked ten hour shifts, six days a week, for a solid year at the Denny's in Burbank. I breathed, ate, and lived Denny's. I became a monster, a monster in a yellow polyester apron. During that year I entered into one of the darkest periods of my life. Every day seemed to bring new insight into the depths of degradation that the human race was capable of sinking to. I started to notice the gluttonous tendencies of the general public. I witnessed their insatiable hunger for butter, fat, lard, gravy, syrup, and sugar. Most people enjoyed their lettuce salad drenched in a mayonnaise dressing, but there was usually more dressing than actual greens on the plate. I noticed the irritated way in which they demanded more potatoes, more beef, more sausage, and more bacon. A lot of people talked with their mouths full, spitting and spewing their food while giving me orders. Their mouths were covered with spaghetti sauce or shiny oil from the fat of the meat they ate. Their teeth were yellow from tartar and tobacco. Their breath was bad from indigestion. They farted into their underpants and belched into their napkins, and in some cases right into my face. I could see it and smell it all. Sometimes after people ate, they would loosen their belts or undo the top button of their pants and try to push the table away from them to allow more room for their bellies to expand, but the tables at Denny's were bolted down. They would stand up and lift the heavy chairs to a more comfortable distance then sit back down, looking as if they had just run a marathon. It was the greed for more and more food. Not nutritious, life sustaining, life celebrating food, but junk food to fill the void in their junky lives. And speed was key. They didn't seem to understand the concept that most of the food they ordered actually had to be cooked before it was served. And this could take some time. I could tell by looking at their complexions that they were used to existing on pre-cooked fast foods. They were used to the quick drive through combo: burger, fries, and a coke on the way back to the office, followed by irritation, constipation, and flatulence. There they were, chomping on McNuggets on the bumper-to-bumper drive home, cussing and spilling their dipping sauce on the car seat. Once safe in their living rooms, the quick phone call to Domino's Pizza, or better yet, a microwavable, frozen pizza, ready in minutes. There's a nervousness to people hooked on junk food. There's an emptiness to the eyes. So short tempered and impatient were these kinds of people that often they would gather their family and get up and walk out the door rather than wait another five minutes for their meal to be prepared. But before they'd leave the restaurant , there would be a quick stop at the register to place a complaint about their waitress for being "too slow" or having an "attitude problem."

As time went on, the different people I waited on started to assume the faces and bodies of animals and beasts. Sometimes I would imagine a combination baboon dog-boy or the face of a swine on the body of a woman, or a group of slothful children inhabiting the bodies of a pack of pit bulls. A group of young girls came in and ordered ice cream sundaes. They each got their makeup mirrors out and started to apply lipstick, eyeliner, and foundation. As I looked at them more closely, I noticed that they were gradually transforming themselves into orangutans. And soon, the vanity of their primping gave way to their prehensile hands picking lice out of each other's hair. The confidence and pride they had had in their appearance, that knowing look in the eyes of popular girls, was replaced by the look of a more trusting innocence of their simian ancestors.

A couple in their thirties came in at the height of the dinner rush hour. I looked at their booth in the corner of the restaurant and cast my eyes under their table. The woman's black panties were around her ankles. The man sitting next to her had his hand in her lap. Over his hand the woman had piled a bunch of paper napkins. I could see his hand in her crotch, steadily working away. They were both staring straight ahead at nothing. It was then that I imagined the whole room, a crowd of pig-faced, monkey-eyed people, some human, some half-beast, some old, some young, all stripping. They all started to take each other's clothing off. Then the copulating began, on the floors, on the tables, in the aisles, in the vinyl booths, and up against the walls. Some used the leather chairs to bend over their partners, some straddled each other on the floor. Old men sniffed out young girls, took them from behind, pumping their buttocks, and screaming. Old women were on all fours being fucked by their husbands. The girls who had turned into orangutans were racing around the room, throwing their own feces at one another. Some were in group arrangements where oral was being performed on one person by several different animals of both sexes. There were sandwiches of people and beasts, threesomes screaming, and groaning, and grinding. They were all making the most ungodly noises. The whole restaurant was full of naked people and animals, fucking and sucking, and grunting. On the bread counter a donkey man had his face buried between a woman's legs. He flipped her over, pulled her ass cheeks apart, and dove his head in. Just then, I felt something wet hit my arm. It was a towel. The manager had thrown it at me. He liked to throw things. "Get these tables cleaned up, girlie," he said, "This place is starting to look like the inside of a zoo cage!"

Open Letter to Sherwood Forest Inn

Sherwood Forest Inn,

Your sign advertises hot fantasies. But before I address the issue of your lack of them, I want to talk about how disappointed I was when I walked into your establishment and found not a trace of Robin Hood, the Sheriff of Nottingham, Maid Marian, Friar Tuck, or even Little John. Nor did I find anything to suggest that your place of business resides on or anywhere near the royal forest in Nottinghamshire or the surrounding kingdom of Northumbria. Your close proximity to Disneyland and Knott's Berry Farm is a dismal substitute for a forest that has been in existence since the end of the ice age. I did not appreciate your misquote of Robin Hood in the sign above your bar, "rob from the rich and give to the whore." Furthermore, your use of the word "inn" perplexes me. This word conjures up a picture of an open hearth. It suggests a place where a traveler can hitch his horse, get a pint of ale, and warm his body by the fire. Where was the mutton stew simmering in the caste iron pot? Where was the fresh baked bread just out of the brick oven, smothered in melting butter?

Sherwood Forest Inn, I had envisioned a room with a bed with a goose down mattress and a woolen blanket. And when I lay my weary bones down to go to sleep I'd look out the moonlit window and see winter's first snow blanketing the ancient Saxon forest. It is a forest of 1,000-year-old oak trees that stand majestically outside the window and stretch on as far as the eye can see.

The hot fantasy would be dreams of the virgin beer maid's bosom spilling out of her bodice and several nude forest nymphs in a forbidden pagan dance at the stroke of midnight.

To recap, my expectations were not met. I had anticipated a magical experience from a place called Sherwood Forest Inn. But all I got was a bowl of stale nuts and a few watered down drinks served by unbathed prostitutes, in a dive that smelled of bacon grease and vomit. I think you'd better change your goddamned name, Sherwood Forest Inn, because I am not about to lower my standards.

Forevermore,

Wendy Rainey

Big Boy

There was a time when the Big Boy Combo,
consisting of the original double-decker cheeseburger,
fries, side salad, and coke,
was the biggest treat in the world for me.
After the meal my parents would wait
while I ran to the fiberglass statue out front.
I climbed up onto the platform
and hoisted myself up by grabbing
one of Big Boy's chubby arms.
I hung off of his neck, pinched his rosy cheeks,
patted his roly-poly belly,
and pretended to pick his nose.
It was a ritual that went along with the burger,
the hot fudge cake,
and the time I spent with my parents.

The other day I noticed this statuette in a store window
and I thought about the times my parents
took me to Bob's Big Boy.
I thought about how excited I'd get when they'd say,
"Get in the car, honey. We're going to Bob's!"
It was as if all of the love I had yearned for from them
would finally manifest at Bob's Big Boy
because they would both be there for me.
And we would be together and happy like that forever at
Bob's

So, after they divorced
I never went to Bob's again.
And when I saw that smiling little statue last week,
I thought, Bob,
you soft, coddled, overfed, ball-less wonder.
You empty-eyed, buttoned-nosed bastard.
I hate those red and white checkered overalls
that make you look like an inbred backwoods hillbilly.
I wish the worst kind of Ned Beatty fate for you
in the most remote corner of the Ozarks
where no one will ever hear your high-pitched squeals.
You are a liar, Bob.
You are a phony and a liar,
and I do not forgive you.

The Glass Eye

He described himself as a black dwarf
with a prosthetic leg and a glass eye.
His name was Derick.
I sat next to him on the bus every morning
as we rode to work in downtown Los Angeles.
One morning he pretended to pop his glass eyeball
out of the socket.
He showed me the eyeball,
and with two other small balls he took from his pocket,
started juggling.
I shouted, "Derick, don't do that! I don't like that!"
He stopped juggling and showed me that the "eyeball"
was really a rubber ball with a pupil painted on it.
I started laughing, and he started laughing,
and all the way to work we were laughing and singing.
And when we got off the bus on Wilshire Boulevard,
and walked toward the overpass,
we saw a swarm of Monarch butterflies.
They flew toward us, and I felt the flutter of their wings
on my arms, and legs, and neck.
I had to shield my eyes as we stood there watching them
fly around us,
and past us, and out over the traffic
onto the 110 Freeway heading south.

Star Light, Star Bright

I was totally freaked out yesterday. I took Brie and Roquefort to a birthday party in the Palisades and saw Bob Dylan there, reading a book in the corner. Anyway, that's not why I was freaked. I was freaked because I saw Ynez Guzman and we talked while we watched the kids play party games, and she told me this story about how when she first started living in the United States she had to live in a tiny room with no real bathroom. It was one of those half bathroom jobies with a sink and a toilet but no shower. She had to wash herself in the sink, one arm and one leg at a time. The people who hired her as a nanny and a housekeeper wouldn't let her use their shower or bathtub, and they paid her half of what she gets paid now. I was all like, "What in the hell? Are you kidding me, Ynez?" And she was all like, "No, I'm not kidding you. I had just come to the United States. I had no money, I had no connections, I needed a job and that's all I could get." I asked her how long she had to work there like that and she told me six months. We sat there awhile without talking. I didn't know what to say to her. I looked at her and I wondered if they were pervs. I was like, "They weren't total freaks I hope. They didn't try anything, right? " I think she was kind of ticked that I asked her that. She's real religious and she doesn't ever talk about sex or anything like that. She goes to church every Sunday and a couple of times during the week to do some kind of volunteer work . She says she wants to be a nun. She's a really good nanny to those kids she takes care of, a natural born nurturer. But the thing about Ynez is that she's had too many bad things happen. She doesn't talk about it but I can tell. Last week I drove all the way up Mt. Olympus to swing by the guest house she lives in behind her employer's house in the Hollywood Hills. I came to drop off the city college catalogue, and she had all this religious stuff in her living room. There was no television or iPod. All she has is a table and two chairs, a few lamps, a photograph of the two blond kids she cares for, her bibles, a couple of shelves of books on childcare, religious studies, astronomy, a laptop, a Smart Phone, binoculars, a telescope, and a bunch of candles, crosses, religious statues, and stuff like that. But it looks kind of cool because she has all these potted plants all over the room and some of them are blossoming and cascading down the rafters and around the pictures of saints and madonnas. And when I looked out her front window I saw the most beautiful view of Hollywood. It was hot that day and when I walked outside to get a better look at the city, I smelled the honeysuckle and pine trees, and I heard the birds chirping and saw squirrels chasing each other, and I looked up into the sky and it was as blue as a postcard. There were no clouds. I could see the moon. A white owl had landed on a branch near the roof. When I went back into her house I found Ynez kneeling at this little altar near her fireplace. I wanted so badly to tell her about the owl I had seen, but I knew she needed to be alone with her God. I saw myself out the door.

Anyway, I was messing with you about the kids' names. The wackadoodles I work for named their kids after wine. I can't tell you their real wine names so I gave them cheese names instead. A lot of the Hollywood people are out of their minds. For instance there was this literary agent I worked for a few years back, I called her "the literary groper." The minute I met her at the coffee shop and saw how she treated the wait staff, I suspected she would be trouble. But I needed a job. Anyway, she had an office on Wilshire near San Vicente and I used to go there to pick up her daughter. The whole place is lined with photos of celebrities, and there were writers milling around everywhere. Inside her office there were a bunch of photos of Morgan Freeman with his arms around her and her daughter. I had no doubt that this hot shot woman knew how to behave herself around the rich and famous, but she sure as hell didn't give a damn how she treated me. Every night before I would go home she wanted the three of us (her, her daughter, and me) to clasp hands in a circle and sing some stupid little song and talk about how magical the day was and all that kind of crap. Well, I went along with it for awhile but as the weeks progressed this freakazoid kept letting her hand get closer and closer to my butt, until one day she was full on grabbing my ass while little Emily was watching. I called her over to the side of the room and asked her what she was doing. And she was all like trying to pass it off as an accident and I was all like, "Hey, I don't want to make a scene in front of Emily, so I'll call you later." So I called her later and I told her I was quitting and she needed to have my paycheck ready so I could pick it up in her office. And I told her she was lucky I hadn't slugged her in the gut. A lot of people would have made a big deal out of what she did but I just wanted to get away from the perv. But the real disturbing thing about it was that I had this feeling that there was something weird between her and Emily. She had adopted Emily from an orphanage in China when she was a baby. Normally I'd think that was a good thing for someone to do, but I thought this woman only adopted the kid so she could have something interesting to tell everyone. It was like the adoption was just another selling point on her resume. She didn't talk to the child like a mother would talk to her daughter. It was more like she thought the kid was a friend her own age instead of just a little six year old. Of course, my gay-dar went off right away with this woman. But, I thought to myself, I don't give a damn if she's gay. She's probably okay. Well, she wasn't okay. And I had a queasy feeling a few times when I had to give the child a bath. There was something sort of sensuous about the way she was behaving. It was like she was trying to please someone. It was only a gut feeling. I didn't have any proof. But don't think I don't wake up in the middle of the night sometimes wondering about that little girl. For about a year after I quit that job every time I'd see an Asian girl Emily's age I would try to see if it was Emily. It never was. And for months I had this dream that I saw Emily in a field. I saw her long, dark hair hanging down her back. I reached out to touch her shoulder and she'd turn around but I couldn't see who it was because her face was sort of pixelated. And then another girl would appear with the same long, straight, dark hair and she'd turn around and she didn't have a face either. And then another girl, and another girl, and another until there were so many little girls they filled the field, but I could never find out if any of them were Emily.

Nancyland

An excerpt from a novel by Wendy Rainey

It all seems like a dream since I made my way out of Nancyland. The world is a different place to me now, bigger and bolder. Sometimes I feel as if I have to grab hold of life right here and now while I still can before my flesh and bone become part of the great compost heap we all must return to when our bodies can no longer endure prison or war or even freedom. Sometimes I still have nightmares about Nancy but I don't give them much credence anymore. It's the humdrum day-to-day details that trip me up. The slapping of thongs, the smell of strawberry preserves, any Beatles song, even the bastardized elevator version can trigger disturbed and restless musings that are a part of a landscape that I myself have created. At one time, the idea of having God's love and protection was meaningless to me. But now, when I see someone lying in the fetal position on the steps of the library, or dazed and speaking in tongues at the bus stop I think, "there but for the *grace of God* go I." It is odd the way certain events can happen in one's life that can change a person forever. Through the Pasadena smog I saw the beast and was confronted with my own animal nature. It was then that I finally cast off the burden of youth and made my way out of Nancyland.

My name is Catherine. This is my story: It was 1999. I was twenty-seven years old, living in Pasadena, working as a waitress, and renting a room in an old Victorian house. Every night I could smell marijuana wafting up the stairs to my room. And every night down below in the drawing room was Nancy, my landlady and roommate. She smoked for medicinal purposes, she told me. She was fifty-nine. She had AIDS. The day before, after I came home from waiting tables for nine hours, Nancy wanted to have one of her talks with me, a powwow, as I later called them. No sooner had I walked through the side door, when Nancy appeared in front of me, hands on hips, wanting to know if we could "touch base." Here we go again, I thought, as I dragged my weary body into the kitchen. She motioned for me to take a seat at her breakfast table, which I immediately dubbed "Nancyland." Plopping into a chair, I noticed the wooden table in front of me. There were burn marks and dents in it. Knife cuts were slashed across it as if she had been butchering raw meat. At Nancy's place at the table, there were hundreds of coffee mug rings stained into the wood, indicating that she had been sitting in the same spot, at the same table every day over the course of decades. She started talking in a concerned and animated way, though I wasn't listening because my hair, face, and body were drenched in perspiration. I could feel the sweat trickling down my back. Water rolled into my eyes. The flimsy sundress I wore looked like a wet paper towel somebody had thrown on my body. I was worried that my breasts were showing through the wet fabric. After missing the bus, rather than wait thirty five minutes for the next bus, I had decided to walk home from work in the 102 degree Pasadena heat. Can't Nancy see what a mess I am, I thought. I took a bandana from my leather back pack and wiped my face. Then I took a water bottle out of my pack and drank from it. Nancy had already been talking for a few moments when I was finally settled down enough to actually listen to what she was saying. I couldn't believe what I was hearing.

"Look, I don't know if you were married before or abused or beaten or raped," she said, "or if you belonged to some cult somewhere. For all I know, you may have just gotten out of prison. I don't know what your *life situation* may have been, but I do know that there is something really wrong with your *interpersonal relationships.*"

"What are you talking about?" I asked, putting my water bottle down on the table. "I've lived here, what, all of ten days? You don't know anything about my *"interpersonal relationships."* I raised both hands to make rabbit ear quotes with my fingers around the phrase interpersonal relationships. You are not qualified to make any statements about my personal life, Nancy. And as far as my *life situation*, that is none of your business."

"Oooohhhhhhhhhh, well, Catherine, I've observed you long enough to know that there is something *very negative* about you." Nancy lifted a mug to her lips: "UNLEASH THE GODDESS WITHIN," it said in large block style letters. "Look, just use the brains God gave you. Most people like a certain amount of chit chat, but you just don't seem to have much in you!" She raised both of her arms and shrugged her shoulders.

"Look, Nancy," I said, sighing and running my fingers through my wet hair, "just use the brains God gave you. I'm a waitress. I chit chat all day long. You know that seven hundred dollars I gave you for rent ten days ago? That represents a lot of chit chat. By the time I come home, I'm all *chitted* and I'm all *chatted* out. There's no more chit chat for you, Nancy, I'm sorry." I started to rise out of my chair.

"Hold on, there are a few other issues I have to discuss with you. Please remain seated," she said. I sat back down in my chair again. She looked at me, adjusting her bifocals, "Ever since you've been living here my Herpes sores have been flaring up. It must be all that negative energy you're putting out there." Nancy made gestures with her thick fingers as if she were popping little invisible bubbles in the air.

"What?" I said, half laughing, although I was starting to feel sick to my stomach. "You're blaming me for your Herpes sores? You can't be serious. Are you joking?" I looked at her. She was pouring herself another cup of coffee from the automatic coffee machine she kept on her table. She had a little canister of cubed sugar and a little pitcher of cream. I glared at her as she doctored up her new cup of coffee. Ignoring me, Nancy charged forth.

"Also, I'd like to remind you that I DO HAVE AIDS and I need to make sure that I get adequate rest, so I'd appreciate you not using the blender at six o'clock in the morning. What kind of person gets up at that hour and puts the blender on? Just stop and think about it. Would you phone a friend at six in the morning? Of course not! It would be entirely inappropriate. By the same token, you do not put the blender on at six a.m., got it? But mainly I want to emphasize to you that your *attitude* is really the culprit here. I'd like to see some improvements over the next few weeks. So think about what I've said. I'd like you to act more like a GUEST in my home. And keep in mind that it is a PRIVILEGE for you to live here, a privilege that I can revoke as I see fit." Nancy took her glasses off and put them on the table next to the burn marks and knife slashes. Then she picked up her mug of goddess coffee and took a sip. I stared at her. She's off her rocker, I thought. Maybe the disease she has is making her insane.

It's a tough break getting AIDS. It's got to be horrible for her. I feel for her, but she's too touched in the head for me to be able to live here for any real length of time. I've got to get away from her, otherwise, she's just going to take her hard luck out on me. "You're free to go now," she said, waving me off. I got up out of my chair. As I walked past her, I was calculating how long it would take to save up enough money to get the hell out of here. I'm sure I can say goodbye to that five hundred dollar security deposit I gave her. She'll find some excuse to keep it. With my modest salary at the café I can probably count on being here for another three fucking months. I grabbed the bannister and started to climb the stairs to my room.

It's strange the way some people seem to change once I get to know them on their own turf. When I called Nancy's phone number from the ad she had placed in the Pasadena Star News, I was relieved by what I thought I heard in her voice; intelligence, competence, and stability. Dizziness overtook me as I entered my room and sat down on the queen-sized bed. It must have been close to a hundred degrees inside my room, even with all the windows open and the ceiling fan on. Falling backwards onto the bed, I started to remember arriving for the initial interview with Nancy and being impressed by her elegant and immaculately kept two-story Victorian home. Nancy invited me outside to look at her vegetable and herb garden. Lemon and orange trees lined the path down to a huge patch of land covered with an abundance of delectables. Twenty-foot sunflowers rose amid watermelon, zucchini, tomato, and strawberry plants. Endive, rosemary, tarragon, thyme, mint, parsley, chives, catnip, lavender, sage, basil, marjoram, garlic, and onions were thriving.

Three avocado trees stood by an old well encircled by stones and mortar. The rusted pump looked ancient.

"It's beautiful," I said, "I feel like Dorothy landing in Oz. Everything's in Technicolor. You must love it here, Nancy!"

"This house was built in 1874," she said, her long, grey hair blowing in the wind. "The property used to stretch all the way down to the end of the block." Nancy pointed to a line of charming bungalows built in the twenties. "This is where the horseman would have lived." She pointed to a well-preserved structure, "It was converted into a tool shed in the thirties. The servant's quarters and stables are long gone, of course. Cows, chickens, and horses were kept somewhere down there." I looked in the direction she was pointing. A kid with a baseball cap turned backwards was balancing a ghetto blaster on his shoulder with one hand, and giving a passing car the finger with the other. She turned around and examined the leaves of a Cecile Brunner. The miniature rose was climbing up a white trellis. "Yes, it was an era when people grew their own food and lived off the land and their wits. She pinched off a brown bud from the rose bush and threw it over her shoulder.

I remembered the first time I sat in Nancy's living room. It was filled with heirlooms. The windows were framed with delicate white lace curtains. A large antique vase contained an assortment of flowers and herbs from her garden. From where I sat I could see two Shaker chairs in the sunlight. "Hands to work, heart to God," I said. Nancy looked at me inquisitively. "The Shaker Creed," I said, pointing to the two chairs. "Oh, yes" she said smiling. She was wearing Bermuda shorts and a white t-shirt. I noticed her white gym socks and athletic shoes. Her bifocals hung from a decorative chain around her neck. "It's wonderful the way you've managed to retain the old fashioned charm. It's like being transported back in time," I said.

"Well, I've made certain adjustments here and there, but the integrity of the original structure has never been compromised. The antiques," she motioned with her hand, "are a passion of mine. I pick them up at estate sales all over Pasadena."

"Nancy, I'm very interested in renting from you," I said. "You have a beautiful house and a lovely garden. The rent is affordable for me and it's also close to my workplace." I looked at her, smiling.

"Now, I want to be absolutely frank with you, Catherine," Nancy said, "I have AIDS. I also had a bout with cancer two years ago, which I survived and recovered from. I have health issues but I am functional, although I do get tired easily. I'm attending Pasadena City College in the hopes of reentering the workforce in the future. If you would like to take a day to think about what I have said, by all means do. Also, the two rooms you will be renting can get awfully hot as you may have noticed. I don't believe in air-conditioning. I've managed to survive here twenty-five years without it. " Putting my ice water glass back on its coaster, I considered what she said,

"I would like to put down a hundred dollars now as part of my deposit," I said, reaching into my bag for my wallet. "I can come back tomorrow and give you the rest of the deposit. I don't have a problem with you having AIDS. And I'm used to the heat. I lived in the desert for three years and I never had air-conditioning." She smiled and looked at me,

"Well, it's settled then. I hope you'll be happy here. I'll get you a receipt for that deposit. You're still welcome to think it over a day if you like."

"OK, I appreciate that. I suppose you might want some time to check the references I gave you." Nancy came back into the living room and handed me a receipt for the hundred dollars I had given her.

"Our meeting here, today, is reference enough for me. The rooms are yours if you so desire."

"Thank you, Nancy," I got up off the divan, "it was nice meeting you." I reached out, shook her hand, and smiled. "I will see you tomorrow after work at around 5:00."

As I walked down the front steps of the stately old house, I detected the intermingling of jasmine and magnolia. Rose bushes lined the long pathway that led out onto the sidewalk. Two squirrels were chasing each other in the grass. I turned around and looked at the sprawling house. An oasis from the madness of life, I thought. Off to the side something glimmering caught my eye, a fountain with a statue in the middle: a cherub spewing water from his little rose bud mouth. He looked as if he was ready to ascend to the heavens.

What a welcome change, I had thought, from the dark, decrepit, vermin infested hovel I had lived in at that time. Mr. Ruiz, the manager, never fixed the dripping kitchen faucet. He never replaced the cracked bathroom window, nor did he get rid of the cockroaches that crawled all over the walls of my apartment. One roach was so big I could always identify her. She stood out from the crowd, a cut above. I named her Coco-Lisa. I tried so many times to kill her, but like so many of her kind, she would not be defeated. The population grew. I set off Raid Bombs, I sprinkled boric acid in the corners of the cupboards, I set up Roach Motels. Nothing worked. I could feel some of my little friends crawling on my face at night. I started to wear a ski mask to bed. It covered my entire head and face with openings for the eyes and mouth only. As spring approached it grew too hot to wear the ski mask. I got a long piece of cheese cloth and wrapped my head like a mummy every night. A white sheet enshrouded my body to complete the look. Eventually, I managed to poison myself with all of the chemicals and powders I was using. One evening, I had to be taken to the emergency room. Finally, I asked Ruiz if he would consider fumigating the entire building, "That way we can nip this problem in the bud, Mr. Ruiz, " I said, "and I can stop poisoning myself." I told him about my trip to the emergency room. "You got poisoned?" he said, oozing with concern, "Oh, my goodness," he gasped, "That is just *horrible*! Heavens to Betsy, are you alright now?" He said the whole problem could be traced back to the Aguilera's two-bedroom apartment. "Those people are pigs," Ruiz said, "Ever since they moved in I've had nothing but trouble from those slobs." He said he would look into fumigating right away, but of course, he never did. But you can bet your sweet ass he wanted his rent on time. And it had to be in cash, no checks or money orders, shady bastard. Every month I would walk across the courtyard to his apartment and knock on his door. And every month he would greet me at the door with beer breath and a gold tooth, wearing his stained, wife beater undershirt. After he counted the cash he would thank me and hand me a receipt for seven hundred dollars. I knew I was being ripped off, but I couldn't find anything cheaper in Pasadena that would accept a cat without an additional five hundred dollars added onto the security deposit and sometimes an additional two to three hundred dollar bribe on top of that. Actually, I was lucky to get the apartment in the first place. If Camila Salgado's mother hadn't died, Camila never would have offered me her place. Camila was my friend from work. Her mother died suddenly and she had to move back into her house in Glendale to take care of her four young siblings. I could tell Ruiz was leery of renting to a gringa, but he trusted Camila, so he let me have the apartment. Well, adios Coco-Lisa and company. Adios Senior Ruiz, you lazy little fuckwad.

About the Author

4th Street Bridge, Los Angeles

I walk along the 4th Street Bridge
inhaling the aroma of garbage and urine.
The cars and trucks zoom by me,
some shouting or honking,
some indicating that they would like to
engage in an act of love with me,
but most just going about their business.
There's always something exciting
about the smell of exhaust.
When I smell exhaust I think about being young
in big cities like New York, Paris, and London.
And if the exhaust fumes are mingled
with just the right measure
of urine, garbage, and perhaps a little human feces,
you can bet your sweet ass I'm in heaven
because then I know I'm in Los Angeles.
And if I happen to see a pile of bloodied clothes
shoved into one of the bridge alcoves,
well, it just gives me that down home feeling, ya know?

Wendy Rainey's works can be found in *Rusty Truck, Chiron Review, Dryland Literary Journal, Silver Birch Press,* and several other journals and anthologies. She is a contributing poetry editor on *Chiron Review,* the founding poetry editor of *Cultural Weekly,* and included in the Special Mention section of the *2016 Pushcart Prize XL Best of the Small Presses* for her poem, "Girlie Show", published by *Chiron Review.*

Hollywood Church is her first book.

www.ingramcontent.com/pod-product-compliance
Lightning Source LLC
Chambersburg PA
CBHW020151180626
46810CB00004B/1839